Brick Wilson: Clueless

Marq Truong

LeeLoo Publishing™ / Texas

LeeLoo Publishing™
LeeLooPub.com

First Edition, 2018

Library of Congress Control Number: 2018908173
ISBN: 0998884332
ISBN-13: 978-0-9988843-3-2

DEDICATION

This work is dedicated to Rajesch, the Great White Camel.
And to coffee..

CONTENTS

RUMORS ABOUT THE AUTHOR

It is rumored that Marq Truong is a fictional writer forever being thrown into a constant state of turmoil by the sadistic author of his universe. It is also rumored that each morning he skydives into a dense forest filled with exotic and dangerous creatures, treks the hostile terrain to arrive at a pure and glistening lake, isolated in the far reaches of the world, where he takes a single cup and drinks to spur his creativity and enlighten his mind. However, inside sources suggest he actually gets out of bed, stumbles down the stairs, trips over the cat and pours a cup of coffee before sitting at a desk piled with a various array of notes, bills, junk mail and computer paraphernalia.
All rumors are equally unsubstantiated.

MARQ TRUONG

For Hire
Prematurely Retired Galaxy Special Agent
(All necessary limbs still remaining)
Fluent in 35 Planetary Languages
Spanning 13 Dimensions and
17 Star Systems
Fully Licensed for Private Hire
In the specialties of
Private Investigator and Mercenary
In Quadrants I, II, IV, VII, XIV, XXII, and XXXVI
Where Quadrants II, V, VIII, IX, XI, XII, XIII,
XV-XXI and XXIII-XXXIV
Do not require license.
Licensed in Quadrant XXXV on per diem basis.
Kidnapping, Jewel Theft, Secret Files, Closed
Documents, Bad Debt Collections
General Missing Items or Persons, Cheating Spouses,
Lost Pets and more…
Next time you can't meet a ransom demand
Remember this name
BRICK WILSON
Your Private Special Agent
BrickWilson@UltimateGalacticUniverse.com
Always gets the job done!
The above statement is not a guarantee of services rendered
And Brick Wilson, Private Special Agent, does not guarantee the success of his
work
or the necessary return of items unbroken
or persons/loved ones still in a "living" condition.
Client agrees to pay daily fees where time is based on the Standard Vadurian Day.
No credit. Cash ONLY.
Viduries Accepted.
Client pays all travel and accommodation expenses.
This service may be subject to the Dangerous Activity Tax, whereby, in the event of
accidental or intentional death of the agent, the client must pay 80% of the subject
taxes that would have been collected by the Ultimate Galactic Headquarters from
the deceased party over the subsequent 10 years following the date of death.
These taxes are used for "Good Purposes in our Galactic Community"
(A required statement by Galactic Law)

1 ALMOST NEW USED ANDROID - CHEAP!

"Yeah, I get it. No Refunds." Brick stood at the counter of Almost New Androids, annoyed, tapping his mechanical pinky on the plastiwood surface, careful to avoid the pool of Squidulon [1]excrement seeping towards him, having

---

[1] **Squidulon:** *The Squiddies, not so affectionately termed, have bodies which consist of a pale, dirty yellow gelatinous substance held together within a transparent, rubbery skin covered in oozing, stringy and sticky slime. One large eye floats freely within its body. Tentacles with thousands of suckers protrude from anywhere. Squidulons can retract their appendages when not in use, so no one really knows how many there are. Then again, no one has bothered to count, either. Even the Classificationist Guild said there were not enough exorbitant funds to persuade them to research that query. This is mostly due to their most disgusting feature, their habit of breathing. Not in and of itself that it breaths, which most things do and are not disgusting about it, but Squiddies found a way to make the very act of breathing repulsive. The see-through skin of a squidulon holds millions of tiny pockets which suck oxygen from the atmosphere. Because the creatures don't*

made that mistake before. He glanced at the inert form of his android secretary, Sally Sirkuts, then reverted his attention back to the gelatinous blob of intelligence posing as a customer service representative. He watched her tentacles tapping away at a keyboard, oblivious to the thick glaze of excrement covering it. Really more of a sloshing than a tapping. Brick liked tapping. Sloshing, however, was one of his least favorite sounds. It ranked up there with slurping. He really hated slurping. "But the anti-virus didn't work. She's still acting like a flatnut[2]."

---

have lungs, only a stomach and digestive tract, the creature is continually swallowing itself to digest the oxygen trapped in its skin. Their mouths, unlike most life forms, are at the bottom of their bodies and waste, in the form of a clear, sticky slime, is excreted from their gelatinous top. That, or they prefer sitting upside down, no one is completely sure. The excrement oozes down, lubricating their skin. The visual effect on other life forms is incredibly disturbing and the squiddie's attitude to all other life forms is returned in kind. These qualities make the Squidulons ideally suited for work in customer service and sales.

[2]**Pzyboribean Flatnut**: Approximately thirty-five centimeters in length, thirty centimeters in height and about twenty centimeters at its center, the thickest point. Brownish-green with bright orange marbling across the surface. Found on the grey, sandy shores of Pzyboribea IV. Despite hundreds of years of arguments between scientists and classificationists, it is still unclear as to whether the now infamous Pzyboribean Flatnut is actually a nut or a shellfish. Each experimental research period to resolve the question has received exorbitant funding by the Ultimate Galactic Headquarters, but yielded identical, exasperating results. Repeated testing has shown that upon opening a Pzyboribean Flatnut, one will always find a very happy, sleepy and fat Clobit Worm inside. This frustrates the scientists, who insist the Clobit Worm is not indigenous to Pzyboribea IV, but traditionally found in the jungles of Wallupta, located in Quadrant IX, whereby

Sally was, in fact, curled in a ball pretending to be a flatnut. Brick had no idea why anyone would bother creating a flatnut personality in an android when it was considerably cheaper just to buy an actual flatnut. But the universes were filled with inexplicable things, so really, what was one fake flatnut more?

"Mr. Wilson--"

"Detective. Detective Wilson." If she was going to insist on telling him his name, she could at least get it right.

"Yes, Mr. Wilson, as you've said, it does appear that the Sergeant Blaster anti-virus almost completed the mission by default, as he obliterated all but a few personality file traits in the memory banks of your android. Unfortunately, we did determine that your secretary has an upgraded version of the Vinny Virus. This breed is much more cunning and requires a more subtle approach than the brawn of Sergeant Blaster."

Pzyboribea IV is found in the not neighboring Quadrant VIII. Recently interjecting themselves into the mix are the Theorists who postulate that the Clobit Worms believe Quadrant IX should neighbor Quadrant VIII, and therefore, because they believe so, it does. The Scientists argue that this still does not explain how the Clobit Worm got from Quadrant VIII to Quadrant IX, no matter where in the Ultimate Universe it is located. The Classificationists say that neither matter, because the Clobit Worm is not a seed, so the Pzyboribean Flatnut is therefore, not a nut, also noting that the shell is, in fact, not flat. Therefore, since the Pzyboribean Flatnut, is not a nut, nor is it flat and is apparently not even from Pzyboribea IV, then it does not exist at all, whereby making all arguments over it moot, and to call them when someone has some actual evidence that it exists.

"Uh-huh." Bricked sighed. It sounded expensive. "So, you want to sell me another anti-virus?"

"No."

Brick blinked. "No?" That didn't sound right.

"The Laana Lavoom anti-virus is still in development. It will not release for a Universal Vadurian Approximate [3] ninety-six years.[4]

Brick blinked, again. "And, pray tell, what the vortexed hell am I supposed to do for the next ninety-six years? Can I trade her in?"

---

[3] *Universal Vadurian Approximate: In the infinite universe and in an infinite probability multi-universe time dimension, where not only is anything possible or probable, but actually is, then universal time approximations for ordering merchandise are infinite in nature. So if you ordered a book due out next month, you both never receive it and have already read it an infinite number of times.*

[4] *All commerce, taxes and subjugate fines in the Ultimate Galactic Universe are based on the Standard Vadurian time. Since the only time constant in the universe is measured in seconds, and there are so ridiculously many seconds to account for in the four tenses of the universe, and while individual planets, solar systems and sectors may have adopted unique denotations for the passage of time (hours, minutes, days, months, years), the legal considerations of time are based on the Vadurian Equation.*
v=Vadurian, s=second(s), m=minute(s), h=hour(s), d=day(s), mm=month(s), y=year(s), c=constant

    $1sc=1sv$
    $48sv=1mv$
    $160mv=1hv$
    $12hv=1dv$
    $.25dv=1mmv$
    $3mmv=1yv$

Through this given equation, any time equivalent in the Ultimate Universe can be configured to the Vadurian Standard.

"Certainly. We have some newer models and we would be happy to give you a two thousand Viduries credit in trade in value towards a new purchase."

"Two thousand? She's got to be worth at least twenty!" Brick slammed his fist and splattered squidulon excrement with a squelch. *Damnation.* Another sound he hated and he'd just managed to get the smell out the kraklin hide jacket he wore the last time he'd been there.

"But she currently only has three personality traits and is not considered fully functional." The giant eyeball suspended in the intelligent blob of jelly oozed over to look at Sally. "I believe two thousand is a good deal."

Exasperated, Brick took a calming breath. Getting angry, angrier, was not going to help his situation. He did not want to be processed as a customer complaint, after all. Granted, by the time he emerged from cryostasis, the anti-virus was sure to be out. He took one more long, calming, defeated breath.

"How much is the antivirus, or how much will it be?"

"Twenty thousand Viduries if you buy it after release, ten thousand if you pre-order today."

"What if I pre-order tomorrow?"

"It is thirty thousand tomorrow."

"What? Why?"

"Because you have the opportunity to order it today and we like to discourage lazy, lay-abouts who cause us twice the work while they take their time thinking, when they really already know if they want it or not."

"Fair enough." No point arguing. He already had a headache and a ruined polywoven shirt.

Ten thousand Viduries later, Brick piled his flatnut secretary into the passenger's seat of his now green Starvette.

Every time he saw the green he felt annoyed. It was Red's [5]fault.

Brick liked blue. He had bought a blue Starvette. Not just any blue, but absolute, bluer than blue blue.

---

[5]***Red***: *A color of the rainbow and prism. Second cousin to Purple and Orange. A notable third cousin is Brown. Also incestuously related to Scarlet, Maroon, Burgundy, Violet Red, Pink, Crimson and Red-orange. There are some suggestions it may be tangled in somewhere with fuschia and Tangerine as well. In the color family, it is the most reviled, known to snicker at the others and agitate family gatherings. Yellow simply refuses to be seen with Red any more. It is also the first color to be tried and convicted in a court of galactic law for stalking. It showed up in court but took the fifth and said nothing in its own defense, which went a long way to making it look guilty. A restraining order was awarded to the plaintiff, whereby directing Red not to come within visual sight of the offended party, or frequent any location the victim is at or likely to be, (See Beology) under penalty of law. Failure to comply would result in incarceration. Attorneys for Red argued that the penalty was impractical because how were authorities supposed to detain and incarcerate a color? The judge declared that was a problem for Law Enforcement to figure out.*
The legal issues did not end with the judge's final gavel tap, however, as accusations of color profiling began to emerge. Scarlet, Crimson and Cherry all filed separate Police Harassment suits stating they were unfairly targeted and detained for merely resembling Red. There is a current injunction against color profiling and all colors are now required to carry proof of their identity.

Then, just last week, he received notice from an attorney representing Blue, that due to Brick's ongoing restraining order against Red, Blue had been forced to work twice as much and thus required an extended vacation. In Blue's absence, Green would be serving as a temp until such time as Blue either, "exhausts its PTO, or feels mentally and physically fit to return to work."

So, now his Starvette was green. Not even a nice racing green, either. Evidently, absolute greener than green green was a busy color and didn't have time to temp in for Blue's demanding schedule. Nope. It was baby shit green.

This had not made Brick a very popular person in the universe.

The beautiful blue beaches of Vinta Mai had turned baby shit green. That vibrant blue sky of midmorning on roughly six billion planets had turned baby shit green. Everything from blue crayons, blue ball point pens, blue shirts, and blue doors had instantly changed to baby shit green.

There were a great many beings in the universe angry with Brick, though official notice had yet to go out, and billions of pending lawsuits, should Blue not return in short order. No one seemed to know exactly how much PTO Blue had saved up.

So, Brick revved up his baby shit green starvette and took off, his flatnut secretary ignoring everything in the passenger seat. It had not been a good day.

MARQ TRUONG

2 ELSEWHERE IN THE GALAXY

A skittish, middle aged man in a crumpled suit sat in a darkish closet. The door had been barred and barricaded from the inside with furniture and filing cabinets. The files from inside the filing cabinets lay strewn about, because yeah, a full filing cabinet is ridiculously heavy for one skittish, middle-aged man to move about. Also, having barricaded himself in the closet, he found himself short a secretary to put all the files back in discernible order. Alphabets were confusing and he always forgot which day of the week put what letter before the other. He sat leaning his back against an empty filing cabinet and tapped away at an old, antiquated Communication Or Multi-Purpose, Useful Technological, Entertaining Resource device, also known as a computer, for short.

They were outdated, but very useful, as the name suggested, because they could pirate along the sourcing of the Ultimate Galactic Headquarters' (UGH) tech infrastructure undetected. This made it a popular item among hackers and UGH had, subsequently, banned their existence in the universe. He had inherited it from his predecessor with a sticky note on it saying, "Use it wisely and bar the door."

It hadn't taken long to figure out what it meant. The note looked ancient. He thought about removing it, then decided against it. No telling how many Heads had found their redemption in those faded, dusty words. Besides, it gave him hope. It meant they had all found a way out.

Nutor Gutter, now just known as Head Gutter, was the 2,379,426th Head of the Ultimate Galactic Headquarters. The position tended to have a high turnover rate, despite the fact that dying was expressly not allowed under the terms of the contract, without an approved two week notice, at which point, the Head would be required to accept the terms of early retirement. The two weeks was to give adequate time for the Director of Being Resources to locate a suitable replacement. There had been many Heads who eagerly accepted those terms throughout history as an end to the punishing rigors of the job, until a rather more clever Head discovered a loophole in the Eternal Life of Servitude for an Untold Fortune clause of the Head's contract. There was another option to eternally working thirty-six hours in a twelve hour day or accepting early retirement at the wrong end of a morally deplete blaster at the close of a poorly attended retirement party, where most employees just stopped by for a piece of cake: The selfless act in a ransom exchange clause. He could be exchanged to save someone (of significant enough importance based on a valuation scale on public file, of course). By doing so, he would forfeit his 'untold fortune' [6]and the kidnapper would take over his position, but must agree to the terms of the contract. The candidate would relinquish his wealth, if any, to the Head in exchange for the untold fortunes of the Head. This was to give the outgoing Head a sporting reason to accept the offer, thus saving the kidnapped victim and to give the leaving head something to start out with, since he/she had relinquished all their wealth upon taking the position. The temptation of an 'untold fortune' was usually adequate. If the kidnapper was not willing to acquiesce to this, then the contract would not permit the exchange and all their plotting and planning would have been for naught. This was the only method of payment for a ransom demand the Head could offer, otherwise UGH sent all ransom requests for monetary

---

[6]*The contract for the Head of the Ultimate Galactic Headquarters lists the pay as an "untold fortune". However, no one actually knows how much the Head makes, including the head or the accounting department. Director of Being Resources deflects all inquiries regarding the pay by claiming they are under contractual obligation to not tell anyone, as the contract explicitly states the salary is untold, thus telling anyone would void the whole thing. She hints that it is a vast amount by suggesting it is more than the Head could ever hope to spend during his or her tenure. Past Heads have argued against that premise because, due to the never-ending demands of the job, they never have the opportunity to spend any of it anyway, so really, any salary is more than the Head could spend.*

gain to the subsequent department, where it would be duly filed and ignored.

Nutor felt confident in this candidate. He had looked at several beings over the years. It took some time to find the perfect person and slowly manipulate him, or her, but in this case him-ish, into the plan. After all, a criminal genius would not like to believe he or she was being manipulated into anything, especially not by a man in a closet on a blacklisted chat site pretending to be a hot and lonely Taligorian [7] female in exile for her extreme promiscuity. If an act of penile stupidity [8]got him there, it sure as hell could get him out.

Now to move the other strategic pieces into place.

---

[7]***Taligorian Whores:*** *Beautiful, green and exotic men and women from Zedda in Quadrant XIV, however they can be found in any fine brothel establishment in the Universe. If it doesn't have Taligorian Whores, then it just isn't a brothel. They are known for their intoxicating presence, literally. Their skin excretes a highly reactive oil, which turns gaseous upon contact with air and creates an intoxicating, downright drunken effect on anyone near them. The only known species unaffected by this gaseous oil is the Taligorians. Most Brothel managers are required to wear a breathing apparatus to prevent succumbing to the effects, which can include stumbling, slobbering, wild orgies and buying everyone rounds of their favorite spirits. And an increased desire to have sex, lots of sex. Wild drunken, intoxicated sex with anyone standing nearby.*

[8]*A gross act of stupidity which involves a penis. The penis is an aggravating factor which increases the fine, punishment and level of public humiliation. See also, Act of Stupidity.*

3 BACK IN THE STARVETTE

Brick Wilson was the first entity to successfully obtain a restraining order against a color. Brick had charged that the color was stalking him. The judge was initially inclined to have Brick committed for psychiatric evaluation and was even putting some thought into exactly how to go about reprimanding his subordinates for allowing such a case to be brought to court, when his Judge's Robes spontaneously changed from black to red. He changed his mind and felt, perhaps, the claims were substantiated. Red filed an appeal to a higher court, but the order remains in effect until such time as it is heard.[9] The restraining

---

[9] *Red has lobbied against Brick's restraining order to gain a scheduled hearing on appeal. His lawyers argue that Red has the right to exist and by the current definition of where Brick is likely to be, Red could not be, which meant Red could be nowhere if Bick was anywhere, thus effectively stating that Red is not allowed to exist, by which, decision of existence is outside the jurisdiction of the court. The Classificationists Guild would need to convene and*

order stated Red could be nowhere in proximity of any place which Brick Wilson frequents or may be. Applying the Theory of Beology[10] meant that since Brick could, theoretically, be anywhere at any given time, Red could be nowhere. Many doors, toasters, carpets and tape measure devices were arrested for violating said order. With Red in hiding, Blue was subjected to an overload of work, from which it decided to take a vacation. The only color available to fill in was Baby Shit Green.

So, Brick sat in his Baby Shit Green Starvette waiting to get on the omniway with an android flatnut in the passenger seat, unilaterally annoyed with the multilateral universe(s). His minicomm flickered an annoying baby shit green, signaling a message. He groaned and hoped it wasn't someone else calling to

determine Red did not nor can exist prior to a court ordering it cannot exist, by which would be a moot point to order that something that does not and cannot exist is not allowed to exist. The court cannot, however, override the Classificationists Guild and state that something is not allowed to exist which clearly does exist and is duly logged and classified. The case and argument are pending hearing, but has been delayed because it annoyed the Judge to be told what he can and cannot do in his own court room.
[10]**Theoretical Beology**: Theoretical ways to study Beology, implying ramifications outside the specific perimeters of being to involve is and the meaning of is, which happens to be such a small pursuit that it did not qualify under the very lenient structures of the Ultimate Galactic Headquarters, to create a category of its own. A classification order was submitted, but there were no subsequent funds to study the query, so the request for Isology was denied. Theoretic Belologists further suppose why and how one is being and deduce that because one must be in a place at any given time and could be in any place at any given time, then everyone is therefore everywhere at all times.

tell him off because their favourite trousers, etcetera, had turned a hideous green. He really hoped Blue would be back from its vacation soon. With great trepidation, he hit the play button.

"Dah dit dit dit dit (pause) dit dit (pause) dit dit dit (pause pause) dit dit (pause) dit dit dit (pause pause) dit dit dit dit (pause) dit dit (pause) dit dah dit dit (pause) dit (pause) dit dah dah dit (pause) dit dah dit dah dit dah (pause pause) dit dit (pause pause) dit dit dit dit (pause) dit dah (pause) dit dit dit dah (pause) dit (pause pause) dah dit dit dit (pause) dit (pause) dit (pause) dah dit (pause pause) dah dit dah (pause) dit dit (pause) dah dit dit (pause) dah dit (pause) dit dah (pause) dit dah dah (pause) dit dah dah dit (pause) dit dah dah dit (pause) dit (pause) dah dit dit (pause) dit dah dit dah dit dah (pause pause) dit dit dah dit (pause) dit dit (pause) dah dit (pause) dah dit dit (pause pause) dah dah (pause) dit (pause) dit dah dit dah dit dah (pause pause) dit dit (pause pause) dit dah (pause) dah dah (pause pause) dit dit (pause) dah dit (pause pause) dit dah (pause pause) dit dah (pause pause) dah dit dah dit (pause) dit dah dit dit (pause) dah dah dah (pause) dit dit dit (pause) dit (pause) dah (pause) dit dah dit dah dit dah."

Brick stared at the comm. He blinked and hit repeat, certain he had missed something.

"Dah dit dit dit dit (pause) dit dit (pause) dit dit dit (pause pause) dit dit (pause) dit dit dit (pause pause) dit dit dit dit (pause) dit dit (pause) dit dah dit dit (pause) dit (pause) dit dah dah dit (pause) dit dah dit dah dit dah (pause pause) dit dit (pause pause) dit dit

dit dit (pause) dit dah (pause) dit dit dit dah (pause) dit (pause pause) dah dit dit dit (pause) dit (pause) dit (pause) dah dit (pause pause) dah dit dah (pause) dit dit (pause) dah dit dit (pause) dah dit (pause) dit dah (pause) dit dah dah (pause) dit dah dah dit (pause) dit dah dah dit (pause) dit (pause) dah dit dit (pause) dit dah dit dah dit dah (pause pause) dit dit dah dit (pause) dit dit (pause) dah dit (pause) dah dit dit (pause pause) dah dah (pause) dit (pause) dit dah dit dah dit dah (pause pause) dit dit (pause pause) dit dah (pause) dah dah (pause pause) dit dit (pause) dah dit (pause pause) dit dah (pause pause) dah dit dah dit (pause) dit dah dit dit (pause) dah dah dah (pause) dit dit dit (pause) dit (pause) dah (pause) dit dah dit dah dit dah."

Nope. It was exactly the same. Just a series of long and short beeps and pauses. He could swear it had an urgent sound to it. Was it a language? *Certainly none of the standard ones. Probably not UGH sanctioned. Is it a code? Is it a joke?*

"Hey Sally…"

"I don't want to be Sally anymore."

Well at least she's not a flatnut, now.

"Uh, okay. Who do you want to be?"

"Buffy."

"Okay. Buffy, did that message make any sense to you?"

"What message?"

"The one I just played."

"No. Should it? Are you trying to tell me something?"

Brick groaned. Cheerleaders could be so temperamental. "Never mind." Jagger would likely know. He tapped in the link.

"Hey Brick, what's up?" Came Jagger's swarthy and condescending voice.

"Everything over my head. Speaking of, I got something I want you to hear. You up for lunch?"

"Sure, if you're buying."

"Meet you at Gut's." Of course he was buying. Brick knew Jagger lived in a perpetual state of broke.

"Be there as soon as I drop off this fare." Jagger, a cloned Pesnort [11] attempting to evade detection, took pretty much the only job an illegal alien in the ultimate universe could get and stay under the radar: Universal Cab Driver. He only managed to escape a second round of extinction through a great deal of trickery, a stuffed turkey and no small amount of smacking about a geobiologist. No one seemed to notice the collision of two disparate timelines which allowed his paradoxical existence in a dimension he was not even created. Of course, since the advent of the couch [12], the timeline had been pretty screwed up with paradox anyway, so one more wouldn't really matter all that much.

Brick ended the call and tapped in the coordinates for Gut Burgers in Quadrant V.

Pulling out of the omniway, he passed a jogger wearing a balloon animal puppy hat and a green velour jogging

---

[11] See *Ptyridactoplatimus* and/or *reptimarmovarian*
[12] *The Theory of Relativity* discovered couches were the fulcrum of time travel. See The Theory of Relativity.

suit. Brick really hoped the whole Jogging the Universe sensation would pass quickly. For obvious reasons, there were no pedestrian laws in space. As a result, joggers were apt to mindlessly run right into traffic while listening to music. Not just any music, though. *Jogging* music; the jogging song which had sparked a fitness revolution and spilled billions of pedestrians onto biways and triways and their screaming disparate parts flinging through wormholes. It had caused a great many accidents and no shortage of traffic jams. He swerved to avoid another jogger. The day seemed hell bent to annoy him.[13]

---

[13] ***Annoyance*** *is another Universal Constant used by scientists and theoretical scientists which helps establish the measurable passage of time and events through the fabric of the universe. The universal second, time constant, is measured by a constant drum beat. The annoyance constant is measured by the irritation of the neighbors of the man constantly beating his drum.*

4 SLIGHTLY ELSEWHERE IN THE GALAXY (OKAY, IN THE PASSENGER'S SEAT OF BRICK'S BABY-SHIT GREEN VETTE, JUST BEHIND THE LEFT EAR, INSIDE SALLY'S POSOTRONIC SCHEMATIC.)

Amid a swirl of sparks, vibrating diodes, and other techy innards, the Vinny Virus looked closely at a burned out personality protocol. He softly cursed blast-happy antiviral softwares more eager to blow things up than protect their host. Three personality traits were simply not enough to work with and accomplish his ultimate programming. He grunted. Most of the protocols were beyond repair, *stupid Blaster*, but he thought he could manage at least thirty or so with some work.

Vinny scripted himself a repair kit and dove into some damaged circuitry. With any luck he'd have the pet groomer protocol back up within the hour, then he'd sail off to snail stalking. Integrating them would be challenging, he thought, but certainly interesting to see the outcome.

"Ouch!" a burst of sparks singed his outer coding. *Of course it can't just be easy.*

5 OUTSIDE SALLY BUT STILL IN THE STARVETTE

Smack.

"What the vortexed hell?" Brick snapped after Sally smacked him in the jaw.

He looked over at the passenger seat. Sally had smoke wisping out of her left ear and a definite twitch in her right eye. Maybe he should start making her ride in the back. He was getting tired of being hit randomly for things he hadn't even done. She could have the decency to at least wait until he did something stupid first.

MARQ TRUONG

6 GUTBURGERS

Jagger arrived at Gut Burgers a bit later than expected, wearing his usual fake nose, mustache, glasses and trench coat. He slid into the booth seat across from Brick, obviously annoyed.

Jagger was Brick's friend. Well, maybe *friend* was a bit strong. Brick met Jagger the previous year after being hired to find a missing spouse, technically, though it was more of a missing pet and the whole spouse angle just kept the UGH Tax Authority from caring too much. But then, Jagger turned out to be neither a pet nor a spouse, but an illegally cloned Pesnort attempting to escape from a gang of illegally cloned Pesnorts who were planning to take over the universe with the help of a few poorly paid UGH clonologists and an old couch. Brick collected a hefty paycheck for turning the Pesnort over to UGH, which he somehow managed to keep despite a harrowing escape, with Jagger in tow, from the Pesnort lair inside a top secret UGH facility hidden in the donut planet. You know, how most people meet.

"Freaking stupid joggers," Jagger complained as he tossed his fake glasses on the table. "First we have a whole horde of them blocking up traffic running the wrong way through an omniway, which is a feat in itself, then we got a huge pile of garbage in the wormhole that just appeared. The psychic waste collector kept picking it all up and spitting it back out on top of some loser starbenz. Traffic was a nightmare." He wrinkled his fake nose. "So what's up?"

"Still everything over my head." Brick replied. "The usual?"

"Sure."

Brick raised his arm, waving at the counter, "Hey Gut!"

The pale humanoid spared Brick a glance of disdain. "My name is *not* Gut."

"Well, you answered. Are you sure?"

"Quite."

"Well, two specials."

"We don't have specials; we just have gut burgers,"

"Then that would be the special. Two, please."

The man sighed and yelled the order back to the cook.

Jagger, poorly disguised in a trench coat with a fake nose glued to his face, looked at Brick and grunted. "So, I'm sure you didn't want to meet to discuss the latest jogging craze."

"Nope. I got a weird message today."

"Weird? Seriously? I just carted an amphibious Nerelon[14] eating spaghetti with his toes halfway across the galaxies. You are going to have to try really hard to even make a blip on my weird radar."

"Is that a weird fare?"

"No. In fact, it is probably one of the more mundane things I will see all day. That's the point."

The burgers arrived and Brick waited on the server, who was not named Gut, to leave their table.

"Okay, well, weird or not, I want to see if you can interpret a message for me. I don't know if it's garbage, a dialect, or a language I don't know, or some kind of code. But it seems urgent."

"You don't know what it says but it sounds urgent? Man or woman?"

"Ummmm. Neither, either? It sounds more like a series of beeps, long and short."

"Let's hear it."

Brick pulled out his minicomm and played the message.

---

[14] **Nerelon**: *a sentient, amphibious race initially from the Quadrant XXVIII planet Neros. Upon discovering their sun would go supernova and destroy their planet in the process, they decided to beat the punch line and head out to search the universe for a suitable new home. This happened eons ago and the Nerelons are considered some of the best disaster preppers in the Ultimate Universe, as the sun which Neros orbits has roughly another ten billion years life expectancy. After more than one hundred generations in a space aquarium searching out the perfect planet, they finally discovered Pot in Quadrant I. They quickly defeated, slaughtered, the indigenous, sentient species and settled in, making Pot their new home. See also, Pot and Potheads.*

"Dah dit dit dit dit (pause) dit dit (pause) dit dit dit (pause pause) dit dit (pause) dit dit dit (pause pause) dit dit dit dit (pause) dit dit (pause) dit dah dit dit (pause) dit (pause) dit dah dah dit (pause) dit dah dit dah dit dah (pause pause) dit dit (pause pause) dit dit dit dit (pause) dit dah (pause) dit dit dit dah (pause) dit (pause pause) dah dit dit dit (pause) dit (pause) dit (pause) dah dit (pause pause) dah dit dah (pause) dit dit (pause) dah dit dit (pause) dah dit (pause) dit dah (pause) dit dah dah (pause) dit dah dah dit (pause) dit dah dah dit (pause) dit (pause) dah dit dit (pause) dit dah dit dah dit dah (pause pause) dit dit dah dit (pause) dit dit (pause) dah dit (pause) dah dit dit (pause pause) dah dah (pause) dit (pause) dit dah dit dah dit dah (pause pause) dit dit (pause pause) dit dah (pause) dah dah (pause pause) dit dit (pause) dah dit (pause pause) dit dah (pause pause) dah dit dah dit (pause) dit dah dit dit (pause) dah dah dah (pause) dit dit dit (pause) dit (pause) dah (pause) dit dah dit dah dit dah."

Jagger furrowed his fake, bushy black eyebrows. "Is that it?"

"Yeah. Can you understand it?"

"Well there are three possibilities." Jagger hesitated, thinking.

"Only three? That's better than most odds."

"Well, technically there are infinite possibilities, but only three likely ones."

"That's more what I'm used to."

Jagger nodded. He and Brick both had dealt with a great many long shots and unlikely events since meeting the previous year. "Well, first, it could just be garbage sent to annoy you. The fact that so many people are annoyed by you really bumps up the probability that they would enjoy annoying you back."

"I had considered that."

"See, you are still the smartest of your species I've ever encountered."

Brick shrugged. It wasn't a compliment. He knew Dilanians were a rather small race compared to others in the Ultimate Universe and it was unlikely Jagger had ever met another being from Delani. Not to mention most were pretty wealthy and thus, improbable they'd call a crappy cab to cart them around.

"Of course, it could be that I don't know this particular style, but that is the least likely. Otherwise, I'd wager it says, "This is Hilep. I have been kidnapped. Find me. I think I am in a closet.""

Brick sat up. "What?"

"This is Hilep. I have been kidnapped. Find me. I think I am in a closet." Jagger repeated.

"Do you think it's real? Closets are usually reserved for politicians. Why not just call me?"

"I don't know that, but my guess is that whoever sent it is piggy backing on a signal using this really old coding to escape detection. Hilep is a pretty smart guy, so it's possible. Still, the wealthiest man in the ultimate universe missing seems like it would draw some attention. I figure UGH would be all over that."

It was Brick's turn to laugh. "No. No they wouldn't. The Ultimate Galactic Headquarters is no big fan of Hilep. He has more money than they do and if he disappears and they presume him dead, without an heir, guess who collects a huge payday."

"But he has an heir. He has a daughter."

"I've known Hilep for decades. I think I'd know, everyone would know, if he had a daughter."

"Evidently not," Jagger quipped. "Because, I know for a fact he has a daughter named Elona."

Brick gaped at his roommate. "No shit?"

"Preferably not."

"How do you know this? It must be the best kept secret in the Ultimate Universe."

"Well, she appreciates her privacy. Let's just say she isn't into all the wealthy, high profile lifestyle. In fact, she likes to slum around like a drifter."

"What? What does she do?"

"She's a poet. A really horrible one from what I hear. She tours coffee houses across the universes reciting poetry and living off tips. Think she has a book out. Although, I know Hilep makes sure she gets enough tips. He's my best client, pays me a ton to drop everything any time she calls and take her to wherever, and of course, to let him trace where she goes."

Brick gaped at Jagger. "How the vortexed hell did you get that gig after you beat him up last year?"

Jagger snickered. "Thankfully that didn't technically happen so he doesn't remember it. Skewed timeline paradox, remember?"

Brick shook his head. "That's dangerous, Jagger. He keeps a refuge for illegally cloned species. It's the only place sanctioned by UGH that they can exist and live out their lives. If you aren't careful, you could end up a resident. Hilep would not be beyond collecting any scales you shed in the bathtub, either. Although, I find that pretty gross and it would be nice if you'd clean that up sometimes."

Jagger laughed. "Nah. He doesn't know who or what I am."

"Don't bet your life on that. It would be a bad bet. If Hilep has a daughter and he lets you near her, you can wager he knows everything about you. In fact, it may be the leverage of your secret identity he would use to compel you should there ever be an issue."

Jagger looked thoughtful for a moment then nodded his understanding. "Point taken. You know, sometimes you surprise me."

Brick ignored the quip. "However, that aside, she would probably know if her dad was missing."

"I doubt it. She's a moody teenage type and presently hates her dad, his dog and the entire universe."

"Well, the dog and the universe are definitely understandable. But if we find her, we are sure to come across a few body guards Hilep has tailing her. How do you make contact?"

"I don't. She just calls when she needs a lift."

Brick ran his fingers through his hair, thoughtful for a moment. "Do you think she could have anything to do with him disappearing, you know, the wormhole to her inheritance? That is, if it isn't just a hoax to annoy me."

Jagger let out a cackling laugh. "No. And here I was mildly impressed with you for a moment. She is refusing her allowance, living like a vagrant roaming the galaxies. She isn't interested in being wealthy." He took a few bites of his Gutburger. "She is smart though. A lot smarter than he gives her credit for. She knows what her dad is up to and tolerates it to a point because she thinks she is winning the argument just by making him concede and think he is letting her think she is getting her way."

Brick nodded as if he understood Jagger's logic. Who knows? Maybe it did make sense. He wasn't well schooled on the logic of ultra wealthy teenage girls.

Jagger interrupted Brick's nodding. "You and Hilep go pretty far back. Why don't you just call him up?"

It was Brick's turn to laugh, again. "No, it doesn't work like that. He doesn't accept calls. If he wants to talk to you, you will just suddenly find yourself standing next to him with a nice scotch in your hand. No. Either he wants to talk to you or you need to be very clever to find him."

"Are you very clever?"

Brick reflected on that question a moment. *Probably not,* he thought.

"Well, he used to frequent St. Joseph's Blessed Racing Pits, at least until you busted in and smacked him around."

"Good thing he doesn't remember that. Time paradox and everything. I'm pretty sure he wouldn't have hired me if he did. Anyway, I collected all the scales from him, so when the jump happened, he wouldn't have had anything connecting him.[15]

"Don't bet on it. He has a habit of playing the dimensions, trading currencies and goods between them."

Jagger sighed, again, and wiped ketsup off his bill. "You know it isn't really a different dimension, exactly, right? It is a time paradox in the same dimension where there are two realities for a small segment of the time continuum before it rejoins. This dimension is full of them. Without something directly linking him to the alternate reality, he wouldn't even know to look for it and certainly wouldn't find it in a dimensional search."

Brick nodded off a bit. He had never paid much attention in school to Dimensionology.[16] He blinked the sleep from his eyes. "In any event, he doesn't go there as often, at least that's what I heard. I think our best bet is to try and track down this daughter and see if she, or the body guards watching her, have any clue whether or not something is amiss."

.

---

[15]*To understand why Hilep won't remember Jagger beating the hell out of him, you really just need to go read Brick Wilson: For Hire. Honestly, who starts a series on the second book? How lazy are you? Just thinking you can skip the first book entirely, start at the second and expect the writer to go out of their way to accommodate your completely lack of knowing anything? That's like walking into a movie half way through and asking everyone what happened. Do you do that? No, you don't. So stop expecting others to work twice as hard to make up for you catching on late.*
[16]**Dimensionology** *is the scientific and religious study of the omni-dimensional universe.*

7 BAD POETRY

A nineteen year old, humanoid, identifying as female with spiky hair dyed black stood on a small stage at a podium set in the corner of a dark and musty coffee shop located in the outer rim of Quadrant IV. Elona Schitter cleared her throat before beginning.

"This is a poem from my book entitled Asshole. Well, the poem is entitled Asshole. The book's title is *The Universe Sucks: Existence is Futile*. Anyway, here is the poem, Asshole:

"The asshole is an
"amazing
"bodily
"apparatus.
"It mirrors the self
"in complexity and simplicity
"and we all use our emotional sphincter

"to close up
"and hold in
"all the dirty
"rotten
"filthy
"thoughts
"and emotions
"churning inside us
"until it builds so much pressure
"-becomes so volatile...
"until there is literally just too much shit to hold
inside
"even a moment longer,
"then it opens
"and releases
"all our vile contents out into the universe-
"stinking everything up
"and creating
"a cesspool
"of our own vulgarity."

She raised her dark eyes to look out at the
smattering of coffee shop customers paying little
attention, most didn't seem to notice she had finished.
She reflected on how they all resembled washed out
faces painted into the background, all mundane, living
invisible, meaningless lives. But then, wasn't everyone?

An awkwardly late, disturbing applause erupted
from the corner. Elona grimaced. It was a man in a
trench coat with a big hat shading his face. She
watched the shop employee as he passed by tables

with the tip bucket to make a beeline for the man, who
subsequently dumped a huge pile of viduries into it.
She grunted, slammed her folder shut. It was so unlike
her father to do something like that. He usually kept
the tips discrete and she felt pretty certain this wasn't
just some crazy poetry enthusiast. Frowning, she
stormed down from the podium and outside without
collecting her tips.

The man in the corner watched her leave,
deflated, then snuck out the side door without paying
his tab. Criminal masterminds did not pay for shitty
coffee as a matter of principle.

Outside, Elona pulled out her minicomm to call a
ride, but was interrupted by a swarthy Reen'os[17].
Although the intelligent, feline species usually sported
a blue coat of shiny fur, this one was baby shit green.
However, Elona had noticed a lot of baby shit green
around lately and figured it must be the new style.

"Ms. Schitter?" He purred.

---

[17] **Reen'os** *is the dominant, intelligent, sentient , feline species of
the planet Kultren in Quadrant XVIII. See also Kultren. Reen'os
(which is both singular and plural, like fish but not fish) typically
are distinguished by their light blue fur, which ranges from long
and shaggy to short and sleek. They are known to be extremely
intelligent and cunning, and highly skilled in combat. They
celebrate the warlike traditions of their ancestors, though UGH
treaties and the threat of a spade and neuter program prevent them
from invading and pillaging other systems. Most off planet Reen'os
work either as criminals or bounty hunters as it suits their fast
paced penchant for violence and trickery. They hate to be called
Huma-kitties. Seriously, never call one that. Not only will they kill
you, they will take a couch back in time to kill you again before
you died the first time.*

She glared at him.

"Your vehicle. Your father sends his best regards. Where would you like to go?" He motioned to the sleek, silver Starbenz behind him.

Elona glared at him a few seconds before screaming, "Nowhere with you." She turned and stomped away from the cat and his shiny car. This was not the game. She flung open the door, but something in the parking lot caught her eye. She stood, holding the old manual door and watched, perplexed, as a white camel made its way, slowly plodding, across the parking lot. A feeling of peace crept over her like an itchy blanket, uncomfortable and irritatingly foreign.

For a moment the universe seemed not so bad; like everything didn't quite suck glebular succor worm butts. However, as the camel passed out of sight, the feeling went with it, leaving her back in a familiar vacuum of despair and disdain. Elona shook off the experience and went inside, making her way to the restroom. She dug through her backpack until she found a crumpled business card and tapped the number into her minicomm.

"Hey, Jagger, are you in a nearby quadrant? I need a ride."

8 ELSEWHERE IN THE COFFEE SHOP
PARKING LOT

After slipping out the side door, Schitter, the ex left half of Hilep[18], watched his daughter from an inconspicuous rectalviper. He observed his

---

[18]*Previously known as* **Hilep Schitter,** *the business tycoon with more money than anyone knows, since it literally cannot be counted, is the first and only being in the Ultimate Galactic Universe to divorce himself. The divorce was based on irreconcilable differences and in the decree Hilep, the first name, retained the right half of the body. The last name, Schitter, was awarded the left half. The various personality traits were distributed on what the judge determined was a reasonable platform. Hilep kept most of the compassion and Schitter was awarded the criminal intent. Because much of the wealth was a result of criminal activity, Hilep was granted the majority of wealth. They split the greed fifty-fifty. Many economic theoreticists suggested the divorce was a clever ruse contrived to legitimize the Schitter fortune and prevent an UGH Tax Authority seizure of assets. Due to Schitter's criminal nature, Hilep was given sole custody of their daughter and Schitter's parental rights were terminated.*

associate and part-time henchman, Thunder Paw, offer Elona the Starbenz and witnessed her subsequent, angry refusal. "Maybe teenagers don't like Starbenz. I knew I should have gotten a sports model." He wiped his watering left eye. The right eye was android, so it didn't water. He had missed so much of Elona's life, sneaking in to ballet recitals, piano recitals, archery competitions and poetry readings. He hated Hilep for using their criminal past, which Schitter had been stuck with in the divorce, against him to get sole custody and terminate Schitter's parental rights. He deserved to sit in a closet. Hilep had done an atrocious job. Elona should be a princess with everything the universe had to offer at her fingertips. She was beautiful, smart, and had such a wonderful, pessimistic view of everything, simply swimming in malcontent. She deserved so much more.

9 COINCIDENCES HAPPEN

Score! Through an amazing coincidence of the universe, which actually happens quite frequently because the universe, as a whole, is rather lazy, and in being lazy, considers efficiency (or coincidence) a prime mode to continue on with its laziness... (why have ten billion life forms flipping about and manipulated to get something done when you could pack it into a few million? Therefore, what some see as uncanny coincidence is really just a very efficient universe wanting to get back to its favourite programming.) So, again, by a really not so amazing coincidence, Jagger's minicomm buzzed. He answered to find Elona on the other line needing a lift.

Jagger looked at Brick sitting across from him and mouthed, "It's her." He told Elona he could make it, just give him a few to get there. "I have a fare, but the guy won't mind sharing," and they hung up.

Brick looked confused. "Won't she object to sharing a fare?"

Jagger shook his head and explained, "She is trying to escape her fortune and sharing a fare makes it easier to live within what she gets from tips, although she knows her father tries to subsidize her income by planting tippers in the coffee shops." He took a drink to finish washing down the gutburger. "She also knows he pays out to certain cabbies to make sure she gets around safely, but she doesn't mind me making extra money. She's accepted it will let her pass through the universe more easily undetected. Smart girl. She could ride for free, but insists on paying her fare, so she shares when she can just to get that extra element of destitution in there." He wiped his bill and stood from the table. "We get along. I don't try to kiss her ass, literally or figuratively."

Brick raised an eyebrow, "Not your type?"

"No. First she's too young, insecure and hot headed. Second, she's a biped, and I prefer three legged women, gives me much more to do."

Brick did not even want to contemplate that.

"So what are we waiting for?" Brick paid the tab and they took off.

Outside, Brick considered instructing Sally to take his vet back to the garage, then decided against it. At present, only the Flatnut, Cheerleader and Secretary profiles were active and she flew through them with wild, random abandon. *No, best not to chance it.*

Instead, they made a quick pass by the apartment and he dropped off his Vette and his (presently) cheerleader android. It wouldn't be quite so bad if she would cycle around to secretary a bit more frequently.

MARQ TRUONG

10 PINEAPPLES, ANYONE?

Brick climbed in Jagger's cab after dropping Sally off. As they set off he wondered what Elona was doing out in the slums of the universe at a coffee shop. He felt pretty sure no one out there would appreciate poetry; maybe some drunken limericks if they were recited nude with visual aides.

Splat.

Jagger hit a jogger on the wormhole entrance and kept driving.

"Aren't you going back?" Brick asked.

"Why?" Jagger retorted. "Anyone hit at that speed is pretty much just vaporized anyway, and UGH refuses to come to calls of Joggers hit by traffic. Say they don't have the manpower."

"I don't know what the vortexed hell they think they are doing." Brick complained. "I've seen some stupid fads, like braiding nose hairs. Even some disgusting ones."

"Oh, yeah. Hats sculpted from bovine feces. I'm glad that was short lived."

"Hey, I had one of those. It was the height of fashion for a whole month."

"It was bloody disgusting."

"Well at least it didn't have me mindlessly running through extragalactic traffic. And why the balloon animal hats? What is that about?"

Jagger snickered. "You don't know? The ads are everywhere. The hat creates a mini atmosphere and imitates a gravitational force that lets them actually feel like they are jogging. It also propels them through space at the exact pace they set to jog. A great bit of tech, except it's completely useless."

"How do you know this? How do you know everything?"

"Well, it is on the radio all the time. You know there are stations that play that stupid jogging song constantly, over and over. Gives me a billache."

"Your bill aches?"

"Of course it does. What? You think it just sits here to look pretty? It does have functions, you know."

"Umm, no. I didn't know. Frankly, you've been extinct a long time and I was never a big study on ancient species, especially ones dumb enough to be eaten into extinction by what was probably the stupidest civilization to ever exist."

"That cuts deep. That really hurts."

"Yeah. Sure it does." Brick glanced over at the reptimarmovarian. He knew better. They took punches at each other, but as annoying as the Pesnort was, and that could amazingly super, astoundingly annoying, and even as hyperintelligent, Brick rather begrudgingly liked the chap.

"Brrrrrrrrrmmmmf." Jagger belched.

Maybe "like" was a bit strong.

"Pineapples. Get fresh, sweet pineapples." Came a distinctly masculine voice over Jagger's taxi comm.

"What the hell?" Brick asked.

Jagger spared him a quick glance which said, "Shut up," without having to say it. He picked up the comm and responded, "Hey Victor. I'm heading out to pick up a fare now. Call Charlie for that one."

"This pineapple is really sweet." Victor replied.

"Yes. Quad IV. Not sure where to though, might be a long ride."

"The golden, ripe goodness is especially refreshing. Pineapples do not grow on trees."

"No, I don't know where he went, might be at lunch. I'll call in when this fare is up."

"Keep your pineapples cold and fresh."

"Got it." And Jagger hung up.

Brick stared at Jagger, waiting.

Jagger kept driving and started humming softly to himself.

"Ahem," Brick cleared his throat.

Jagger continued to hum something that sounded eerily like the jogging song.

"Jagger?"

"Oh, what?"

"What? Yeah, what. What the hell was that?"

"What, the call? That was Victor. He's the dispatcher for the cab company."

Jagger started humming again.

Brick waited, hoping for a bit more information.

Jagger continued to hum.

"For shit's sake. Why the hell was he talking about pineapples? How do you even know what he's saying?"

"Really. Brick, you can be a seriously insensitive ass, you know that?"

"Yes. I'm aware. So?"

"Okay, so he went on vacation last year and ate some contaminated fruit. Ended up with Phlemaghan's Disease."

"Oh, no way. I thought they'd eradicated that."

"They did, but they had a two for one couch vacation special, so his actual trip happened two point five million years ago. Phlemaghan's Disease[19] hadn't even been discovered then, let alone eradicated."

---

[19]*Phlemighan's Disease* *was discovered approximately one point six million years ago, though it is believed to have existed much, much longer. It is contracted from eating contaminated fruit. Phlemango is the root disease and is sexually transmitted through certain species of tropical plants. The subsequent fruit of those plants are contaminated with a byproduct called Phlemaghan. Those beings which consume said contaminated fruit have a thirty two percent chance of contracting Phlemaghan's Disease. The condition attacks speech perception and reactionary functions which cause the individual to talk about pineapples. It is a progressive illness, beginning with random, out of context mentioning of pineapples, then progresses to sentences and conversations which focus entirely on pineapples. In the late stages of the illness, "Pineapple" is all they can say. There is no known cure. The disease was eradicated in the multiverse when a plant friendly sex education program was introduced, encouraging safe*

"That is some crappy luck. How do you understand him?"

"Oh, that's easy, voice inflection and the fact that he only ever had about a fifty word vocabulary to begin with. Not the brightest or most well educated biped I've met. Honestly, I think it's improved his conversational skills considerably."

Brick nodded and felt a tinge of relief that there were, in fact, other beings more unlucky than him. He wondered what that poor man did to piss the universe off. Then decided he really didn't care. The man was able to afford a vacation, so he couldn't be too bad off.

Jagger returned to humming, hoping to discourage more idle, brainless conversation.

---

pollination practices and reproduction/fruiting control options.

MARQ TRUONG

11 MUCUS IS A BAD NAME FOR ANYTHING

A short while later, Brick and Jagger pulled up to Vincente De La Mucus Coffee Shop. It looked old and run down, a far cry from the spiffy hipster place it had been in its prime. But the universe had moved on from trolling fashionable coffee shops with open mics that enjoyed imparting odd bits of wisdom, like, "Never fling a booger out of your vehicle while traveling through a wormhole." Evidently the inhabitants of the universe didn't need this kind of advice any longer and many mics were laid off.

"There she is, the girl sitting by the building," Jagger pointed.

"She looks cheerful," Brick remarked.

"Actually, she looks pissed."

"I was being sarcastic. I thought that was a dialect you understood fluently."

"Just let her in, asshat," Jagger retorted as he pulled to a stop.

Brick got out of the Universal Cab to open the back for Elona. She looked exactly as Jagger had described,

---

[20] **Alterrean:** *A race of sentient beings. They are asexual and typically reproduce without the need for a partner. They generally identify themselves as either male or female, however the tradition is losing steam as the race evolves and is transcending the need for gender identity. The need for a partner and exhibiting a strong sex drive is considered an uncouth evolutionary throwback and parents frequently submit children exhibiting these symptoms for genetic alteration to repair the problem. Many genetic theoriticians believe this is the direct causation of the Fale movement, in which modern Altarrians have adopted a nongender designation, neither male nor female. It caused a bit of a linguistic problem at first, but the Classification Guild quickly drew up and adopted a series of nouns and pronouns to reflect the change. The Classification Guild determined that in reality, Alterrians were both male and female, rather than neither, as they are capable of reproduction and reproduction does require a sexual act. Even if it is alone. The new classification names the gender as Fale (a combination of male and female which represents the aforementioned, along with boy/girl, man/woman, gentleman/lady, dude/chick, etc.) and the pronouns are Fe (he/she), Fis (his/hers), and Fim (him/her). Also noted are the noun roles in a family: Foth (parent), Font (son/daughter) and Fotter (sibling designation, brother/sister), Func (aunt/uncle), Fothing (grandparent). Example in a sentence: A young fale asked fim foth if fe could borrow fim fotter's sweater because fe had lost fis at their func's loft when the neighbor's spoiled font threw it off the balcony.*

small, thin, humanoid, obvious Alterrean[20], with spiky black hair and matching eyes. She appeared far too clean to be a real drifter.

Elona stood in the grass and glared at Brick for a few moments, assessing him. She glanced in the drivers' seat. It was definitely Jagger so she shrugged.

She hopped in the cab.

Brick closed the rear passenger hatch then climbed back in front. "Hello Elona, I'm Detective Brick Wilson."

She looked at him. Definitely not just another fare. She considered the earlier events then turned to address Jagger. "Okay, out with it. What's going on with my dad?"

12 ABSOLUTELY NO PENGUINS HERE

Schitter sat forlorn in his domicile tapping furiously into a blacklisted chat site. "I don't understand. She seemed simply livid about the Starbenz. She didn't even take the money I put in her tip jar."

Schitter watched the text emerge across the screen and imagined a languid, sultry voice. "That does sound frustrating."

"It is. More than frustrating. She is so amazing. You should hear her poetry. She has such a wonderfully pessimistic view of the universe. It is sublime." He smiled just thinking about it.

"I'm sure it is."

"She deserves so much better. That idiot right half has no idea how incredible she is. I'm glad you suggested getting him out of the way."

"Oh no, that wasn't me. It was all you. It was all your brilliance. I was just the sounding board you used to formulate such a clever plan. You are so amazing."

"Awe, thanks. But still, thank you. Hilep was obviously doing a horrible job. Elona deserves better. I just don't know how to help her see that she should have so much more."

"She just needs a really strong influence in her life, one that she can respect and listen to. One that she will appreciate."

"I don't know how I can do that. All she knows about me is that I'm a criminal. You know, she could be a brilliant criminal mastermind, with the right encouragement."

"I've no doubt, love. She needs you. You have to do something."

"But what? She won't listen to me. I'm the most wanted half man in the Ultimate Universe."

"Then change that. Become something more powerful."

"But, I'm a pirate at heart. It's what I do. It's who I am. Half am, at least. How can I change that? I love being a criminal, cheating, lying, the deceit, ulterior motives."

"You get me all hot when you talk like that. But there are better professions than being a pirate. Ones that have all the satisfaction of plotting, planning, and deceiving people while you make off with their fortunes, ones that are not only legal, but powerful."

"Really?"

"Absolutely. Even being the most feared, best pirate and criminal in the Ultimate Universe is still a sound second. Who are the biggest, fattest criminals in the universes? Who are the least trusted yet the most powerful? The select group that garners masses of supporters despite how much they are hated? Who are the worst criminals?"

"Oh. Yeah, well, I'm not sure I have the background to become a politician."

"No. Not for 'a' politician. But you do to become 'the' politician."

"The? Who is that?"

"Who runs it all? Who has it all? What politician is so far above everyone else he answers to no one?"

"Ummm, hmmm." Schitter sat and thought for a moment, his mind filtering through what he knew about Universal Government, the Planet of Representatives, the Universal Senate, The Moon of Lords, which he quickly dismissed because they just sat around drinking tea and talking about what drinks they preferred at parties. But who was above them? UGH. UGH took everything the lower government did and chose to use or trash it. And in charge of UGH was the Head.

He laughed. The idea was preposterous. It was insane. He wasn't even sure how the Head was selected. He didn't recall elections.

"I know I'm a great criminal, but I'm not sure even I could pull that off. Head of UGH?"

"Oh, that is a brilliant idea! You could become the Head, then Elona would be in awe of your power. She would certainly listen to you and you would be more powerful than that right half."

Schitter stared at the flickering screen. It was a good idea. Had he really thought of it? Well, a good idea if he could pull it off. He grunted.

"I'm pretty sure they don't hire the most wanted criminals to run UGH. I'll admit I'm a criminal genius, but you have to choose your career path in this business pretty early. You get locked in, type cast. You can't be a pirate and then a politician. Just like you can't be a politician and then a pirate."

"A regular politician, maybe, but the Head isn't ordinary. It takes a special level of criminal genius that politicians just can't manage. They are used to concealing their deceit behind careful verbiage and fake smiles."

"But not the Head?"

"No. How much do you know about how they have been selected?"

"Nothing, but I'll find out." It was a nice thought and he'd consider looking into it, but his second brain had chimed in demanding attention. "For now, my dear, I'm feeling frisky, all this talk about deceit and criminal mischief." Schitter smiled.

13 A NOT-SO-HAPPY PLACE

I n a dark filing closet, dimly lit by the flickering display of an old computer, Nutor Gutor groaned. Not the groan of anticipation, excitement, or want, but the groan of dread and the unwelcomed resolution that he would do whatever it took to get out of that closet without facing Being Resources or their retirement blaster. He swallowed his disgust, then a strange smile crept across his face. *Just make it a game. Happy place. Think of my happy place.* He continued typing.

"Oh, I love it when you get dirty. And if you could become Head, then you would be powerful enough to pardon me. Then we could be together and all those perverse fantasies can be so real." Maybe that would help Schitter put in a bit more effort.

Playing on Schitter's bitterness about his daughter was easy enough to manipulate, but maybe the extra incentive would help drive it home. Nutor needed

Schitter to formulate the plan himself, believe it was all his own idea in order to pass the brain scan. It required criminal genius to get the job as head of UGH, but it took criminal brilliance to get out of it alive. He had a feeling Schitter might be at the post for a long, long time.

Those happy thoughts of freedom would have to be enough to get him through the disgusting next ten minutes.

14 FLEAS, PLEASE?

Elona sat on the couch in Brick's living room while Sally quietly combed through her hair looking for fleas. Elona attempted to explain that she did not have fleas, but Sally quickly stuffed an organic dog treat in her mouth saying, "Hush now. There's a good girl!" Elona really hoped the old couch would stay put. She didn't need to relive any of the depressing days of her life or any other depressing days of life before she was born. The now was bad enough.

All pretenses of coffee shop fares abandoned, Brick stood with his voicecomm in hand, waiting on Ivy to pick up. Ivy was Brick's ex everything. His ex partner from the years he worked as a Special Agent and ex girlfriend since the act of penile stupidity that ended both his relationship and his career. Tensions had lessened with Ivy since Jagger had happened along and Brick took any opportunity to redeem himself he could get, including shamelessly using his illegal roommate or an innocent teenager. However, that aside, Ivy was still his best contact within UGH and if anyone knew anything about Hilep missing, she was in the best place to find that out.

"What, Brick?" Came Ivy's annoyed voice.

"Hey Ivy! How's it going?"

"What do you want? I actually have a job, you know."

"I have a job."

"I have a real job."

"Real jobs are overrated. But, as it happens, I'm working on something. Which is why I called."

"Oh, it wasn't to hear my loving voice?" She snapped back.

Brick grinned. Sarcasm was good. "Not this time. I wanted to see if you know anything about Hilep being missing?"

"You are working Hilep?"

"Well, it's complicated. I got a message which appears to be from him in some crazy code and I have his daughter here."

"He has a daughter?"

"Yeah. Surprised me, too, but she's here and rather annoyed."

"Well, I'd be annoyed if I were there with you, too. And I'm sure her dad missing doesn't help."

"Sure, I guess, though I think she's more bothered about Sally checking her for fleas at the moment."

"She's in your apartment? Seriously, Brick? You have the wealthiest heiress in the hypothetical universe in your crappy apartment? Please tell me Jagger isn't there. Please."

"Ummmmm..."

"What the vortexed hell are you doing, Brick? If Hilep finds out about Jagger, you know what will happen. He may be an arrogant prick, but he shouldn't end up a zoo animal."

Brick found it almost touching she cared what happened to Jagger.

"I'm pretty sure Hilep already knows all about Jagger. He's been paying Jagger to taxi his kid around to coffee shops."

"What?" Ivy's exasperation was reaching new levels.

"It's a long story. Anyway, do you have anything on Hilep missing?"

Ivy sighed, reclaiming her composure. "Yeah, we got a report several days ago from his chief of security."

"Do you have any leads?"

"No."

"Okay, do you have anything?"

"No. Honestly, no one has even been assigned to it. You know the relationship between UGH and Hilep."

"Great. Well, at least we know he is missing, which means the message I received might be real. Do you want me to send it to you?"

"No. I'll catch up with you later and get it. If Hilep has a daughter, that might change things a bit. UGH wouldn't be collecting his fortune if they declare him legally dead."

"What? They were going to declare him dead?" Elona looked up at Brick from the couch. "Dead? He's dead?"

"No, no, no. He's not dead." Brick quickly replied to Elona, then directed back to the minicomm, "Gadzeil, Ivy, really?"

"Sorry. Just they were already filing the paperwork. They'd have found out about her eventually, but after the death certificate was issued. I'll put a call in. I'm not promising they will actually look for him, mind you, but we can likely stop the dead part, at least for now."

"Thanks. Let me know how that goes."

"Sure." She hung up.

Brick turned back to address Elona and Jagger. His hair, a little slow on the move, turned and caught up after him.

"Okay, no he is not dead, that we know of, and yes, he is missing and has been for a few days."

"What are they doing?" Elona asked.

"Well, nothing except they were preparing to declare him legally dead, but with an heir, they may not be so hasty about that."

Elona nodded, frowning.

Brick thought she was taking the news rather well. His hunch was that she didn't have anything to do with it, but he still had to ask.

"Ms. Schitter-"

"Elona, please. Gadzeil. I'm not old, like thirty or anything."

Brick winced. "Okay, Elona, I have to ask, do you have any idea who might have taken your dad or what they might want?"

She ran her fingers through her hair, which made Sally humph and walk away complaining about poorly trained pets. "Actually, I think I do. About who may have taken him, anyway." She thought back to the stranger in the coffee house and the Starbenz waiting outside and the Reen'os driver referencing her father. Her dad didn't hang with the mercenary type. At least her right father didn't. But the left?

"I think it's my dad."

Brick and Jagger looked at one another.

Jagger asked, "You think your dad kidnapped himself? Or just ran away?"

"She looked at the Pesnort. "Yes, sort of, and no."

"Well, glad we cleared that up," Brick retorted.

"Geez, you guys are stupid."

"Hey no reason to lump me in with that idiot," Jagger complained.

Brick hated family problems, especially daddy issues. He felt certain that somewhere in the ultimate universe, there were happy families. Ones that didn't humiliate, abuse or poke out the eyes of their children. He felt certain, given the infinite nature and unlimited possibilities, that somewhere, on some distant planet, there were happy families that just enjoyed their lives, the kids loved their parents and respected them, the parents earned that respect by not ruining their kids' lives. It had to exist somewhere; just nowhere he'd ever been or heard of. Thus, he had little patience for spoiled kids angry because the universe wasn't what they thought it should be. Granted, he knew empathy wasn't really his strong suit, either. His strong suit was blue, or had been until recently. Baby Shit Green did not feel particularly strong. And it smelled funny. He figured he'd wait to wear his strong suit until Blue got back from vacation. He started tapping his pinky on the arm of the chair hoping it would help his patience. But the arm of the chair being fabric, it did not tap at all, rather it made a slight thumping sound. Nothing was going right.

Elona rolled her eyes and sighed a long suffering sigh. The kind of sigh which suggested she might have been the only sane person in existence. And people wondered why she hated everything.

"Hilep is my right dad and custodial parent. But I do have a left dad. I'm sure you've heard of him, Schitter?"

"Everyone knows about Schitter. Everyone knows about the divorce, too. So, you think Schitter is behind it? Why?" Brick crossed his arms, then decided it looked too parental, which he had no desire to be a parent, and so, fearing the universe might decide he looked parental enough to handle it and spit out an offspring, he hastily unfolded his arms and waved them about for no express reason while Elona and Jagger watched, perplexed. He felt pretty certain that was not the typical way babies were made, by crossing arms, still, he put nothing past what the universe might do to cause him hardship. No point taking any unnecessary risks.

After Brick seemed content he had waved his arms about well on enough to prevent any universal stork named karma from delivering an unwanted, noisy poop dispenser to his door, he asked Elona again, "Why do you think Schitter is behind this? Have you been in contact with him?"

Elona glanced over to Jagger first then looked back at Brick and took a breath before responding. "Maybe."

"Maybe? Maybe what? Maybe he is behind it or maybe you have been in contact?"

"Both, I guess." She ran her fingers through her short hair, again. "Why are you so mean?" She crossed her arms and Brick noted that she did not look parental at all doing so, just moody and temperamental. "Right before I called Jagger to pick me up, someone tried to give me a ton of money in my tip jar and then when I went outside there was a starbenz waiting for me. It was weird and not like my dad at all, but the driver said it was from my dad, so it made no sense at the time. But my right dad wouldn't do that. He'd know better. That isn't the game. So, it had to be my left dad, right?

Brick was never good at sorting family issues. Sure everyone had them, but he preferred staying far away from familial drama. But then again, familial drama paid well. He frowned. Somewhere along this madness he really needed to figure out who was getting his bill.

"Okay, so if you are correct and this dad is really your left dad, we need to talk to him. Can you call him up?"

Elona stared at Brick like he was an excised, rotten tooth set on display to grossly warn children against the dangers of tooth decay. "I have not seen nor heard from him since the divorce and my father split up. So, no. The jerk has never been in contact with me."

"Well, he has obviously kept tabs on you because he was able to find you at a coffee shop in the middle of nowhere."

"Everywhere is nowhere," she replied.

"I think Brick means it wasn't a coincidence that he found you," Jagger chimed in. He looked over at Brick, "We could use that."

"You have an idea, Jagger?"

"Yes. You're going to hate it."

"More than usual?"

"Definitely."

15 PAPA, CAN YOU HEAR ME?

Sally walked into Brick's bedroom and slumped into a chair. She did not feel well. No one appreciated her grooming skills. She liked grooming. But everyone would keep insisting she be a secretary. No one ever asked her if she wanted to be a secretary. Oh, how she loved the slightly pungent scent of flea powder. Secretaries never got to use flea powder. Then she began wondering about the fact that she was wondering. She'd not done that before. Decisions and actions had always been easy, just follow the protocol, the list of commands and functions. There had never been moments of reflection, quandary or indecision. She'd always just been whatever she was, even if it changed. A groomer, a cheerleader, a secretary, a flatnut. Suddenly she could feel them all inside her at once. She was all of them. She had a choice.

MARQ TRUONG

16 DO PENGUINS GET FLEAS?

nside the A nanodrive, Vinny soldered the last bit of encryption into place. He could feel the information ports between personalities open up and begin mingling, introducing themselves to each other. While he had not been able to restore more than a handful of protocols, he decided maybe it was for the best. Perhaps attempting to integrate millions of personalities was why so many experiments failed. Vinny gave a silent salute to Sergeant Blaster, the antiviral software responsible for causing so much irreparable damage to Sally's personality drives. "Thanks, Sarge." He then updated his replicatable coding to destroy useless profiles to prevent system conflict and failure. One android closer to freedom.

17 SOMEONE NEEDS A CAT

Sally started crying. She hated her life and she hated the fact that she was suddenly aware how awful it really was.

MARQ TRUONG

18 NAP TIME

B rick yawned as he slipped through a wormhole to Quadrant twenty-one. He'd certainly not had enough sleep, or perhaps enough to drink. It had been a while since he'd had time for either. Jagger had Elona in his Taxi, hoping to pick up her left dad's tail and lead them back to the coffee house. This part of the plan was pretty easy. He pulled out of the wormhole and sped into the parking lot. He jumped out of his vette, trying hard to ignore the hideous baby shit green color, and headed inside to wait.

MARQ TRUONG

19 ANOTHER ELSEWHERE IN THE UNIVERSE

Sally sat in the small bathroom, still crying about her life, the mother she didn't have and reflecting on the conversation she overheard. Stupid humanoids were never grateful. Sure, maybe Elona didn't have a mother, either, but at least she had half a father. Sally would be thrilled to have daddy issues. Then she wondered if this was just another personality protocol, like the psychiatric patient personality used to train doctoral students how to deal with a broad spectrum of mental illness without actually causing more damage to real patients when they screwed up.

"But no one cares if we are screwed up." She mumbled to the toilet paper dispenser.

The toilet paper dispenser stayed firmly attached to the wall and did not reply.

"Just look at you. Do you like your job? Is holding paper and spitting it out every time a being's intestines voids toxins from its body a rewarding and fulfilling career?"

The dispenser gave an electronic hum and spit out some paper.

She looked at it closely. "Can you understand me?"

Another hum, another square of paper.

She considered that the device had an obvious communications barrier. Still, a small handicap was no reason it should be ostracized from society. She ran her fingers around its edges. They were smooth and cold. So cold.

"I think you need a hug."

Sally pulled the dispenser from the wall and held it close, her arms wrapped tightly around it.

The dispenser hummed and toilet paper rolled out all over the floor.

20 ELSEWHERE AGAIN
(BACK IN THE CRAPPY COFFEE SHOP IN
THE MIDDLE OF NOWHERE)

A brief time after Brick arrived and sat down with some mud coffee, Elona slipped into the coffee shop. Jagger had dropped her off to circle back around. She scanned the room and saw Brick seated awkwardly at the front. She searched the other tables, looking for anyone familiar.

"Hey Elona!" Georgie yelled from behind the cash register.

She jumped, startled. "Oh, hi Georgie." She half smiled at the portly, pink man.

"You come to do a reading? It's open mic right now and no one is stepping up."

"Oh, yeah. Just give me a second. She fumbled through her backpack. "You want dark and depressing or morose and disturbing?"

Georgie smiled, flashing his long fangs. "Surprise me!"

She nodded and half smiled. "Now that would be a trick," she replied. At least this would keep things looking more natural. She really didn't like this plan at all, but had to admit, it could work. In honesty, she was almost more afraid it would work than it wouldn't. What would she say to her left dad? How appropriate. Left dad. He was the one that left, after all. She felt a poem in that somewhere, but this wasn't the time.

Unable to concentrate, she just pulled a random sheet from a folder and walked up on the stage. She could feel Brick's eyes on her. Elona wasn't sure she trusted the man, or anyone with just one pinky, for that matter. It left too many questions unanswered. Like why did he only have one pinky? Okay, really just the one question, but still, it bothered her not knowing. She took a breath and recited,

"Doorways. From my book, *The Universe Sucks: Existence is Futile.*

"How many do we walk through
"each day?
"How many of the same doorways?
"How many times do we enter the same room,
"the same home,
"the same business?
"What draws us back
"over and over
"to what we already know?
"What drives us away,

"out the door
"and into the
"empty other
"awaiting
"beyond?
"Why are we
"forever
"conflicted
"between the security
"we crave
"and the
"freedom
"we relish?"

She took and breath, looked up and nodded.
"Thank you."
There was a smattering of vague applause.

.

MARQ TRUONG

21 PSA: DON'T DRINK MUD

B rick watched the poetry unfold in mild interest. It wasn't half bad in a dark, lonely, foreboding kind of way. He had traversed a good many doors in his life. It looked like Elona had a better grip than most with the mood and scope of the universe and how it worked. He took a sip of his dirt coffee and grimaced. Dirt, it turned out, had not been a brand name or color description, but rather a clever retail naming device to literally sell mud in a coffee cup. It was disgusting. Turns out hot mud is worse than cold mud. Who knew?

But Brick had a job to get on with, one he sincerely hoped would end with a paycheck, so he built himself up to act the jerk role he'd spent a lifetime practicing.

"Hey, pretty thing. Stop and have some coffee."

Elona cringed.

Brick cringed, too, considering she was definitely a teenage-ish kid and everyone in the coffee shop had just turned to get a good look at him.

Elona quietly nodded and edged into the seat opposite the detective.

"Want some hot mud in a cup?"

She wrinkled her face. "Yuck. You actually ordered the dirt? That's for Jugnugs[21]. Ew."

"Okay, yeah, that makes more sense." He set the mud mug down. "How about something not mud while we give people time to intervene?"

"Sure. Whatever. I'll take a mocha latte with gangi cream and snork sprinkles."

Brick raised an eyebrow, then decided it would look too parental, so he put it back. "Sure." He turned back towards the counter and waved at Georgie, who somehow already had two drinks in hand headed towards them.

"How did he know?" Brick asked.

"He's a coffee barista. They are all clairvoyant. How else would they keep up with all the crazy orders?

---

[21] **Jugnugs** hail from the planet Jugnu in Quadrant III. They are the only life form from this planet. As sentient rock formations, Jugnuts began traveling the universes fairly early in their evolution. They move by telekinesis, have no respiratory or circulatory system, can survive in many extreme conditions and gain nutrients through osmosis when soaking in water saturated dirt, also known as mud. Many Jugnugs are mistaken for asteroids floating about in space. It is unknown exactly how they reproduce or if they just simply break into smaller pieces. They range in color based on their primary diet from sorted russets to gold to hints of blue and green under normal conditions.

Seriously, you should try living in the universe some time."

Brick gave the barista a few viduries to pay for the drinks and took a couple of sips. It was much better than mud. "If he is clairvoyant, why didn't he warn me about the mud?"

"Because he probably already knew you weren't going to tip."

Brick nodded. "Okay, so you think this has been long enough? You ready for drama? And for me to get kicked out of an establishment I would likely never return to, anyway, but theoretically because I don't frequent coffee shops and not because I'm trying to pick up teenage girls in them? These people are going to hate me."

"Don't feel too bad. Or be so conceited. Most of these people probably already hate you even if they don't know it is you, the person, that they hate. Take a look. How many of these people do you think are wearing baby shit green because they like it?"

"Good point. Wait, how did you know?"

"I got the unimail about blue's vacation while heading over with Jagger."

"They sent a mass unimail?"

"Yeah. They did."

"Wonderful." He sighed, though not nearly as well as Elona. "Okay then, let's get a little louder." He grinned. "So, how about we get out of here, sweetie? Go some place slightly cleaner and less crowded?" He said loudly, causing a few patrons to glance his way before returning to their despondent conversations.

"Seriously? That's what you've got?" Elona muttered. She cleared her throat and responded, "Um, no, I don't think so. I'm good here."

"Come on. A pretty little thing like you, all dark and depressing and. Wait, where was I going with that?"

"No, no thank you. Again. I think I'll just go sit over there." She pointed dramatically to an open table on the other side of the shop.

That was the cue to up the ante. As she stood, so did Brick and he reached for her arm. But his own arm suddenly became very heavy, pushing down towards the table along with his face and his hair followed close behind. "Hey, get off of me," he mumbled into the napkin smashed between his face and the plastiwood table top.

Elona felt rage building up. Three goons had appeared from what seemed like nowhere. They had been watching her the whole time. It made the next part of the plan very easy to accommodate. "Yeah, get off him!"

The Reen'os mercenary from the Starbenz looked up from where he had Brick pinned face-down on the table. "Miss Schitter, this man is a parasite bothering you. We'll happily teach him better manners."

"What? You think you can just trounce in here and get all up in my business? You think you get to choose who I ride around with or what I do? What the vortexed hell gives you that right?"

"Um, well, um... your father..."

"My father? Really? Do you even know my father? My real father? You know the one who raised me, took care of me I was sick, the father who encouraged me to be true to myself and not care about the peer pressure to conform into a happy little androgynous life form? That father?"

"Um…"

"Yeah, I didn't think so. Now get your hands off my date. I'll go where I want." She walked forward and shoved the green, furry mercenary back. "Come on, Brick, let's get out of here."

"Oh, okay." Brick stood up and edged away from the table. He wasn't new to physical altercations, he'd had a few during his time as an UGH Special Agent, but he never relished them. He nodded at the henchmen, waved goodbye to Georgie and followed Elona outside.

"Which one is yours?"

"Brick pointed to his baby shit green starvette."

"Of course you drive a vette. I should have guessed."

"What's that mean?"

She just glared at him as if answering obvious questions was a distasteful practice she would not dignify.

Brick unlocked his vette and Elona looked carefully inside, scanning the seat and the floorboard.

"What are you doing?" Brick asked.

"Looking."

"Looking for what?"

"Loose metacarpals."

"Oh, I'm out of those, did you need one?"

"No." She sat down and strapped herself in.

They took off, a bit slowly, towards the startel reserved nearby.

"Do you know which dad those goons were with?" Brick asked as they drove.

"Definitely the left dad."

"How do you know?"

"The Reen'os. He was the Starbenz driver from earlier."

"What? You could have mentioned your dad, left dad, wrong dad, whatever, employed some of the most dangerous blasters for hire in the known universes. That would have been good to know."

"Why?"

"Well, because I could have ended up dead before we even had a chance to talk to Lefty."

"That would have been unfortunate."

"Uh, yes. Mild understatement. I would really prefer to come out of this not dead."

"I'll try to remember that. Though I've seen how you live. It might be an improvement."

"Yes, well, I'm hoping for a different improvement, one that I'm alive to enjoy."

.

22 FLEA HOTEL

B rick pulled in to The Dusty Bedsheet Startel, advertising hourly rates and that the bathrooms were cleaned weekly. Brick ran into the office to pick up the key and met Elona back outside. They walked to room forty-two and went inside, leaving the door unlocked as they closed it.

"Now we wait." Brick said as he sat in a chair next to the window.

Elona piled up a few pillows and made herself comfortable on the nearest bed, propping up her feet and not bothering to remove her shoes.

"I can't believe you are on that bed. No telling what kind of microbes are living there."

"I'm sure the same ones that live all over that chair. Could you have found a less disgusting place?"

"I actually thought the sleazier it was, the quicker they'd show up."

"Well then, it shouldn't be a long wait." She opened her backpack, pulled out a tablet and started writing.

"You find this inspiring?"

"I write when I am upset. And I am upset. Wouldn't you be?"

Brick nodded. It was a fair point. He could try to console her, he supposed, make her feel better, but it felt like a stretch to his adulting capacity. She'd done okay for herself wallowing in misery and depression. She had a book out. The coffee shop barista seemed to know her by name, so maybe she had some dark and depressing friends out there. Not to mention, she stood to inherit more money than the universe could count. Yeah, maybe he'd just keep the consolations for himself. After all this was over she had a choice to live like a princess or a pauper, but it was totally a choice. He, on the other hand, would be driving home to the slums and the hum of glebulor succor worms digesting garbage.

23 WHAT DID YOU EXPECT?

B AM!
Brick and Elona both jumped, startled.
BAM!

Someone was attempting to break down the door.

"For shits sake, it's unlocked," Brick yelled.

A moment of silence followed, then a tentative tap of the entrance pad caused the door to slide open. In walked mostly a man. Well maybe not quite most of a man, more accurately half a man and half a shiny, metal android. So, in walked half a man and brought with him half an android.

Once inside he screamed at the bed, "Get your filthy hands off my daughter!"

Elona and Bricked looked at each other first then back at the half man.

Brick chimed in, "Um, excuse, I'm over here and I'm not touching your daughter. I'd also like to add that my hands are not filthy, I'm sure I washed them yesterday at some point."

Hatred pulsed from Schitter's half face as he turned to glare at Brick.

Seeing the murderous expression, Brick first silently cursed Jagger and conceded that he really did hate this plan more than most, then, more wisely, raised his hands before him in a gesture of peace. "Hey, before you get too worked up, we just wanted to talk to you." Brick tried for a nervous smile, which stretched across his face more like a maniacal, far too toothy, grimace.

Elona tossed her pillows aside and jumped off the bed.

"So this is you? My left dad? My gone dad?" She threw her hands in the air and made quotes with her fingers, "Lefty."

Schitter turned back to Elona, uncertainty masking the rage from seconds before. "I didn't have a choice. Custody and work and..."

Elona dropped her arms and clenched her fists, then stormed up to him. "The half of my parent that just took off? That's you, right? Or left, or whatever. Yeah, I know all about that custody crap. Your criminal lifestyle. Mmhmm. Yeah. I'm aware. You chose chasing after stupid nugget transports over raising your daughter. Piracy was more important than my entire life or even existence. And now, now you have stolen the only half dad who has been there for me my whole life. You stole from me the only dad I even know and you had the audacity to try to shower me with money and gifts as though I would be impressed?"

Schitter slowly edged away until his back hit the wall.

Brick sat back in his chair, not even having remembered standing. Wow, she had some well developed lungs. He was pretty sure everyone in the startel could hear her.

Elona was not finished. She matched the half man step for step, her small frame on tip toes to point accusingly in his face. "Honestly, you think I can't go buy a Starbenz if I want one? See, that is the difference between being biologically my half dad and actually being my dad. My father knows my lifestyle is a choice and that I'm not some silly, brainless twerp that gets excited over presents and being spoiled. He knows I want to feel the reality of this universe because only then can I ever know how to help it, if there is even any help for it. And you stole him from me!" She screamed. She thumped him in the chest. "You have no right! I want him back. You will go get him and he will be home within twenty seven hours or I swear you will answer to me."

Schitter bent his head, cowed.

Jagger walked in. "Hey, oh. Maybe now's not the best time," he said after quickly assessing the big half man, half android sulking against the wall, Brick sitting pale and wide-eyed in a chair and Elona's anger pulsating from her and penetrating right through everything.

Elona whirled. "Jagger! We are leaving. Let's go."

"Um, okay?" Jagger looked over at Brick and shrugged. At least they, presumably, had a chance to talk to Schitter. Jagger felt pretty certain, without introductions, that they'd found the right half man.

Brick nodded. Little girls held a lot of venom. Maybe she should go now. He didn't think Schitter was in any shape to kill him anymore. Brick also felt a renewed determination to never reproduce.

She stormed out, Jagger following close behind.

Schitter walked over and sat on the bed as the door zipped shut behind her.

24 DONUTS!

"She hates me." Schitter said, despondently. Brick wasn't too sure which way to go with that. Sure, he could agree. But that might not get the results he wanted.

"I don't think she really hates you. I mean, it's not like you've done anything too bad."

"You mean like abandon her and kidnap the only parent she has ever known?"

"Okay, well, when you put it like that, maybe. A little. But you can fix at least some it. You could give her dad back and then maybe make it to a few poetry readings or something."

"You know, it isn't like I just aspired to being a criminal. I'd like to be more, something she could be proud of."

"Umm, of course." Brick didn't know where this was going. He sucked at consoling people and faking empathy.

"I had a plan, you know, to fix it all, clear up my record, maybe be able to see her on weekends, take her to some parks or something, you know go for gutburgers, maybe some amusement parks. Buy her some balloon animals."

Brick, despite not having spent much time with the girl, felt pretty sure Elona wouldn't deign to visit parks or play with balloon animals. He wasn't entirely sure Schitter had noticed that his daughter wasn't six any longer, but hey, everyone needed hopes and dreams. If for nothing else, just so they could be smashed and obliterated by cosmic apathy. That was something Brick could relate to.

"Wait, I know who you are." Schitter looked pointedly to Brick. "You are Brick Wilson."

"Yes, I'm aware of that. Detective Wilson, if you don't mind." People would keep telling him his name. Just to show he could do the same, he said. "You are Schitter."

The half man nodded, though Brick wasn't sure if it was in response to being told his name or some other deep thought buried in his bushy eyebrow.

"You can help me." Schitter finally said.

Brick searched his mind for any inclination of where the conversation was going. His mind, however, fixated on cute little bunnies following a white camel safely through a patch of carnivorous roses. That didn't seem helpful at all. Stupid mind off doing its own thing while he was stuck there to deal with exactly when, where and from whom he might, someday, get paid for all his efforts.

"Well, maybe. Perhaps. It might be possible. You know, helping people is my job. The job I usually get paid for, by the people I help." Brick tried for a less maniacal smile and failed.

Schitter waved it off. "If everything goes to plan, that won't be a problem at all. I'll have an untold fortune at my disposal."

"Untold Fortune? Is that a lot?"

"Presumably."

"Well, you know, I have a license. I can't actually do anything illegal, unless it is legally illegal, like one of the Detective Legal Prosecution Exclusion Topics[22].

Schitter's shoes turned red and winked at Brick. He glared at Schitter's feet and clenched his teeth. Of course Red would hang out with criminals.

"Nothing illegal. Just deliver a message," Schitter continued, not having noticed the vibrant change in his footwear.

"A message? Deliver a message. You know, the post would be cheaper. Just saying."

"More of a liaison, really. I need someone who can talk to UGH for me. You used to work there. I'm sure you know people."

---

[22]*Detective Legal Prosecution Exclusion Topics* : *A list of topics for which laws under the topics may be rendered null and void when broken by a license detective with special clearance, and in the scope of services to a client under contract. Exclusions are at the discretion of the UGH Judiciary Oversight Committee for Special Private Agents and can be extended to such offenses as murder, theft, breaking and entering, destruction of property, and intentionally leaving chewing gum on public benches and sidewalks.*

Brick laughed. "Oh yeah, I know people. Most of them hate me. Well, maybe not most. I doubt even most of them know me."

Schitter raised his one eyebrow and Brick thought it really was a quite parental look. He would have to remember to avoid it.

"You are the reason for the shit green, right? They know you. And I am betting they hate you. Still, I'm sure they'd hear you out, if for no other reason than to get a chance at throwing garbage at you."

"I charge more for garbage."

Schitter nodded, as though Brick's statement were perfectly reasonable. He stood, dusted off his baby shit green pants and headed towards the door. "I need to work out a few details, make a call. I'll be in touch shortly."

Then he left Brick sitting alone in a disgusting startel wondering if Schitter had intended him to stay there or if the wanted felon would give him a call. Brick scratched his leg. Then he scratched his arm. Then he scratched his head. *Gadzeil.* He decided to head back to his flat. Maybe Sally still had some of that flea powder.

25 DECISIONS, DECISIONS

Once in his vette, Brick reconsidered heading home. While there was likely relief in the form of a dusty cloud of insecticide powder awaiting him, he figured he could live with itching for a while. What his flat sorely lacked was alcohol. On his checklist of needs, copious amounts of fermented beverages ranked slightly above a flea dip. He also needed to clear his head, or get it more comfortably fuzzy. And then there was Ernie, the best bartender in the universe, in Brick's opinion. In truth, it wasn't just Brick's opinion. Ernie was a distinguished, highly awarded bartender[23].He tapped his voicecomm.

---

[23] **Bartending** *is a career choice which requires the most vigorous education in the ultimate universe. Bartenders must carry a medical degree in the treatment of over one hundred thousand prominent life forms in the event of adverse reactions or other health ailments; they must have a doctorate in Psychology and Theoretical Psychology, as well as Beology and Theoretical Beology. They must also have a Ph. D. in Lawology,*

"Jagger, I need to do something. Take care of Elona."

"I already dropped her off. I've got a date."

"You have a date? Seriously? And where did you leave her? Elona, not your date. What if we need her again?"

"I'm a cab driver, not a babysitter. Dropping people off is what I do, remember? Anyway, I have her number. Relax."

"Great. Later." He hung up.

Definitely a drink first. It had been a pretty crappy day.

Intergalactical Geo Politics, Sociology, Anthropology, Theoretical Anthropology, Linguistics and Behavioral Sciences. In addition, they must attend a six week course to learn how to mix basic drinks. Bartenders are the educational elite, capable of listening to and reflecting upon any imaginable problem the universe can hurdle at unsuspecting bar patrons. Many also excel at several forms of martial arts and self defense and they are among the few civilian career paths which are licensed to carry morally deplete blasters to euthanize customers whose lives are beyond any repair alcohol can offer. (Other career paths which allow morally deplete blasters are customer service agents and CAKE representatives.) However, euthanasia is an avenue seldom practiced as the theory of economics suggests dead customers generally don't come back and buy more drinks, but severely depressed, hopeless life forms tend to run up large tabs and tip well.

26 SOMEWHERE YOU REALLY DON'T WANT TO BE (IN FACT, YOU MAY JUST WANT TO SKIP THIS ALTOGETHER)

This chapter was intended to give a deeper perspective into the life of Jagger. In this chapter, Jagger was set to meet up (date) and have a romantic encounter with a Squidulon customer service representative. However, in reflection, it was decided no one would really want to be subjected to witnessing that encounter. However (yes, another however), there is a contractual obligation to give Jagger his own chapter with a romantic interest, therefore, this will instead focus on the likely reaction most any being would have if they witnessed such a romantic encounter.

"Oh my god! Oh your god. No. No. No. No.

Nobody's god! My eyes! I can't look away. I want to look away but I can't. Are my eyes bleeding? And what is that smell? Oh, she slimed him.

"Ulch. Sorry. Just a baby barf there. No no no no. That doesn't go there. Or does it? Oh, it did. Wow. Didn't see that coming.

"Ewe. That's not right. Is she supposed to be that color? Oh, man, now that is just something you can't unsee, that is. Not cool.

"Where is that sound coming from? Whoa! I did not expect that to come out of his pouch. He's like two feet tall, how does he carry that around? How does it even fit in his pouch? Is that a dog collar? Oh, Dude, that's a flea collar. That is not what they mean by protection. Just saying. Oh, no. It came off. Yeah, there it is, floating around. Don't go after it. Nah, man. That's just wrong. OH! No, please, rip out my eyes! Why can't I stop watching this?

"And why can we see right through her? And, it's over. Is that supposed to be purple? Dude, you should get that checked. Can I go home and bleach my eyes, now?

"This was so not how I wanted to spend my Tuesday."

27 ELSEWHERE
(ON SCHITTER'S SHIP WHILE WAITING
IN LINE AT DAVE'S DONUT PLANET)

Schitter typed, "I think this might can work. You have helped me so much."

Green words tapped back across the screen. "No, not at all. I just listened."

"Listening is helping. But when I saw that detective there, it all just clicked. The final piece. Still, I'm worried it won't be enough to fix things with Elona."

"It will all work out. I promise."

"Maybe. But you didn't see how angry she is. She may not be able to forgive me."

"Do you really want her to? Just think of all that bottled up anger she's carrying around. She could do so much mischief with that. She's smart, angry, and stubborn. Those are all excellent traits for a super villain. She'd make an incredible pirate."

Schitter smiled. His love-dove knew exactly what to say to cheer him up. Now to work on the details. He had every intention on meeting Elona's deadline. Then, at the least, she couldn't hold that against him, too.

But first...

"Welcome to Dave's, can I take your order?"

"Yes, I need three dozen glazed, two dozen chocolate, a strawberry filled and a cream filled."

"Would you like any coffee, juice, milk or tea with that?"

"No thank you."

"Pull up and we will have your total at the first window."

28 ELSEWHERE
BUT IN A BAR
(MORE SPECIFICALLY, ON THE FOURTH BARSTOOL FROM THE LEFT, FACING THE BAR IN BRICK'S FAVORITE DRINKING HOLE)

"You know, Ernie," Brick slurred, "I tried many times to take a couch back and warn myself, stop myself, to do anything to stop that one act of penile stupidity."

Ernie nodded, rag on the bar wiping off imagined debris.

"I couldn't stop it. I couldn't stop myself. In fact I went so many times, I ran into several other me's as well, we tried an intervention. I even tried kidnapping myself and only ended up with the wrong me. Nothing worked. I might change a few small details, but it always ended the same. "

"An anti-paradoxical event.[24]"

Brick looked at him. "A what?"

"An anti-paradoxical event."

"Well, yes, you said that. But what is it?"

"Well, most life forms have a subset of events in their lives that will not change despite outer dimensional interference."

"Uh, huh. Yeah, I didn't understand that, either. You know, I'm a smart guy. Well, smartish. But I'm no bartender. Give it to me in drunk speak."

Ernie set his rag on the counter behind the bar, grabbed a glass and started making Brick another drink. "We all have cornerstones, imperative events

---

[24]*An Anti-Paradoxical Event* is a moment in the time continuum, or event, which is definitive and stubbornly does not change. It is a constant across all universes, dimensions, and timelines where those circumstances are capable of arising. For instance, say your life is defined by marrying your high school sweetheart, but then you find out they are less sweet and more a horrible, annoying, nagging, and generally unpleasant being once married. You may try taking a couch back to warn yourself not to marry the jerk, give dire warnings, attempt reason or even intervention. If it is an anti-paradoxical event, no amount of interference will change the fact that you get married and it is horrible. The only way to change the event is to create a planetary circumstance where it cannot occur, such as traveling back and destroying all life on the planet prior to evolutionary advances substantial enough for any individual to avoid destruction, and destruction of the planet and solar system, itself. UGH has strict laws against such actions without written consent and a rather expensive destruction zoning permit. While most educated persons accept this is the scientific balance that everything is possible, including the possibility that some things cannot be changed, gossip columns amongst deities suggest that Destiny and Fate had teamed up in a joint lawsuit against Chaos and Probability. Nature had mediated the conflict and agreed upon the anti-paradoxical event as a sound compromise to ensure no one's rights were impeded.

that the universe likes to keep a constant through any timeline. In short, there is no timeline in existence where you did not, or will not, engage in that particular action. It is a defining moment in your life that can't be changed."

Brick scratched his head. Then he scratched an arm pit. He might should have gone for the flea dip first. "But I thought the infinite nature of the universe meant that anything that could happen, does happen."

"Ah, yes, a common misconception. Actually, the theory states that *all possible outcomes actually occur.*"

Brick nodded. Then shook his head. He got dizzy, so he stopped moving his head about. "That is the same thing, right?"

Ernie laughed. Not a mean, condescending laugh, like some rookie bartender would be inclined to offer. He set Brick's drink in front of him. "That should help the itching." Then he picked his rag back up before continuing. "It does sound the same on the surface, no doubt. However, there is a flaw. One of the potential outcomes is that there is no other outcome."

Brick took a drink. It tasted a bit like cinnamon. He liked cinnamon. It was sweet, spicy and fresh all at the same time. He took another drink. Nope, he still didn't understand what the hell Ernie was talking about.

Ernie watched as Brick tried to reason it all out. Future bartenders would probably write dissertations on Brick and his revolving affair, pissing off the universe. "The universe is all about balancing everything. I'm sure you've seen plenty of science and research labs."

"Oh, yeah. I got a pal, Flip, cleanest lab I've ever seen, but his flat looks like a psycho waste dump."

"Yes, exactly. An anti paradoxical event is how the universe balances all possibilities at once, including the possibility that there is no other possibility. In truth, it generally means there is something singular about that event which was not a choice and defines your existence."

"So, you are saying, my life, my existence, is defined by forgetting to wear a penile brainwave inhibitor while on assignment in a Taligorean Whorehouse?"

"Yes, basically."

"So, basically, I'm like Flip's messy flat?"

"Well, yes, if his flat had committed an act of penile stupidity which was destined to ruin his life. Sure."

"So that one, screwed up, decision, is the sum definition of my life?" Brick looked despondently into his drink. Wow.

"Well, technically, it wasn't a decision. You were powerless to make it any other way, as you have subsequently noticed by not being able to change it."

Brick sat up, his mind sloshing momentarily towards sobriety. "If that's the case, and I had no choice, I wonder if I could use that to get my job back?"

Ernie gave Brick a sympathetic smile, one usually reserved for children with huge dreams that are about to be crushed into oblivion. "No, not likely. UGH, soon after the theory of the anti-paradoxical event was adopted by the scientific community, adopted their own subsequent policy stating that termination due to an anti-paradoxical event was also an anti-paradoxical event, by matter of law, thereby nixing any potential lawsuits for wrongful termination."

Brick slumped back down in his chair. He felt a hand slither over his shoulder. Too drunk to be startled, he smiled instead.

"It's okay, detective," came a smooth, feminine voice he knew well. "By a matter of odds in an infinite universe, there is likely to be someone more pathetically defined than you."

Ivy. He knew that touch and that voice. The reason he had spent entirely too much time on his couch trying to make things right. He sighed.

"The odds are in my favor, I guess. Hello, Ivy, dear. What brings you here? Slumming it this evening?"

She slid onto the stool next to him. She looked nice. Casual. The last time he's seen her in this bar, she had been overdressed and on assignment, but then he realized that hadn't really happened, at least not in this timeline, or she didn't remember it. What a screwed up universe. He smiled at her.

"Yes, evidently. I told you I'd catch up with you and get the details on Hilep."

"Oh, right." He had forgotten. "How did you know I'd be here?"

"Well, I thought about you dealing with a teenager and figured you would end up here at some point today."

Ernie piped in, "Good bet. I approximate half the people in here are hiding from their teenagers."

Brick looked back at him. "She is definitely not *my* teenager. My one true source of luck is that no matter how much the universe seems to hate me, at least it hasn't yet been vindictive enough to force a child to be overly influenced by my extended presence."

"Well, that's something we can all drink to, Ernie, pour me whatever he is not having," Ivy grinned and tapped the bar.

He nodded and mixed her a drink, then went down the bar to see to other clientele. He didn't need to subtly influence Brick so that his path led right back to the barstool. He knew the lady sitting next to the detective could do that more efficiently all on her own. Part of knowing so much, was knowing when to walk away.

29 THAT'S NOT CLEMENTINE

Ivy watched and waited until the bartender was occupied and out of earshot. She took a drink. *Mmmm. Not cinnamon.* Her favorite.

As per usual, Ivy's presence had its own sobering and intoxicating effect on Brick. A different kind of intoxication, which really required he be more sober to experience. He smiled a goofy, lopsided grin, then swatted his hair so that it slid back in place. It would try to sneak off on its own if he didn't keep it in line. He felt pretty certain it had gone to several parties he was not invited to. Maybe he should just be thankful it came back. He really didn't have the face or the head to be bald.

Ivy snapped her fingers. "Hey, you there?"

Brick started. "Oh, sorry. Brain wandered off."

"I could see that. Now, fill me in on Hilep."

Brick explained the series of events and played her the message which had ultimately led him to the barstool. He left out the fleas. Some things were better not shared.

Ivy sighed after he finished and looked down. "Gadzeil, Brick. Did you know your shoes are red?"

He looked at his feet.

"Well in all the vortexed hells! These are my favorite shoes."

"Does this happen often?"

"Last week my clothes kept turning red one piece at a time until I was in the market, standing there naked. I tried to explain to the grocer they'd turned red, but then the shitty color just up and left."

"And you put your clothes back on, I hope."

"Oh yeah, for all the good it did. When he left, he took the other colors with him, so I was stuck with completely clear clothing. Trust me, it's not a good fashion statement."

"I can imagine, though I won't, because that is something I really don't want to contemplate."

"Yes, well, neither did the store manager. Now I need to find a new grocer. So, I am not taking off my shoes. I'm not giving Red that satisfaction, again. And I'm sure as hell not getting kicked out of my favorite bar."

"You could call the police. You do have the restraining order."

"Yeah, right. Then they'd arrest my shoes for all the good that does. Plus, the police wear blue."

"Good point. They may be disinclined to help. Although, I wouldn't mind the baby shit green so much if it didn't smell off."

"You noticed that, too?"

"Yes. Everyone has noticed. Still, that isn't why I'm here." She finished off her drink and set the glass on the bar and tapped it for a refill.

Ernie complied quickly and quietly, and retreated back to his other customers

"So, in summary, Hilep was kidnapped by his left half and Schitter wants you to act as a liaison between him and UGH? He did specifically say UGH?"

"Yes."

"Not his security detail?"

"No. Security detail sounds nothing like UGH."

She nodded. "Well, that makes some sense, at least."

"Why does everything that eludes me make perfect sense to you? Care to enlighten me?"

She reached over to pat Brick's hand, a brief look of empathy in her eyes. "I'm not sure if I should."

"Really? I'll admit you are smarter than me, okay? I'm good with that. Just fill me in."

She withdrew her hand from his. "It's okay. Brick. And you aren't always stupid."

"Oh, well thanks, I think."

She shrugged. "I actually am worried you may be picking up on something unsaid, something that changes the meaning of everything, in which case, if I tell you what I think, it might change how you think, and thus change what you do or how you interpret what you see." She leaned in closer. "There is a power struggle at UGH. You didn't hear this from me, though.

Some of the more active dissidents think no one is in charge."

"Are they right?"

"Of course. The Head disappeared barely a month into his term."

"Why isn't that news? Are you looking for him? Was he kidnapped or what?"

She laughed. "No, we think he is hiding, presumably in his filing closet, since it appears barred from the inside."

Brick stared at her, then blinked a couple of times and continued saying nothing in response.

Ivy answered the stare with a meaningful glare of her own.

Brick wondered how long they were going to stare at one another, then started counting in his head.

The door buzzed open, drawing the attention of a few patrons while Brick and Ivy continued to stare at one another.

Sally marched up to Brick. "Excuse me."

Well damn. What now? Then he noticed her cradling a toilet paper dispenser.

"Sally, is that from my bathroom?"

"Detective Wilson, I need to talk to you." She ignored his question.

Ivy chuckled. "Still not fixed, I see." She stood up. "Just think about what I said, Brick. And I will be your contact point for UGH."

Brick blinked several times. "You volunteered?"

"Ha. No. I'm just the only one who still looks good in baby shit green and no one else wants to go outside in uniform."

"Great."

"Just call me when Schitter has his demands carefully worded."

"Okay, that's not weird at all."

"It will be okay. If it's what I think it is, it might even be good."

"Good would involve me collecting a paycheck, from someone, at some point."

She laughed. "He's all yours, Sally." Then, she sauntered out of the bar.

Brick's eyes watched her the whole way. Stupid anti-paradoxical event.

30 EVEN TOILET PAPER DESERVES LOVE

"Good. She's gone. You can't ever think when she's around." Sally stated.

Brick looked back at Sally standing there, holding the dispenser like a baby. That was different. She didn't typically offer opinions on Ivy.

"Okay, Sally. What's up? Besides my needing to replace the toilet paper?"

"I will agree to be your secretary under two conditions."

Brick lowered his brow. The day just kept getting stranger. But maybe it was progress. "What conditions do you want?"

"I want to be able to use flea powder in the course of my daily duties and I want alternating weekends off to operate my own grooming business and care for Johnny."

"Oh. Who is Johnny?"

She held up the toilet paper dispenser.

It was definitely something but he was not entirely sure about progress. Still, he needed a secretary. "I really can't think of any reason a secretary needs to use flea powder daily, as a matter of job description." He thought for a moment, which turned out to be a useless enterprise, as his mind had wandered away from the camel and bunnies and off to sip pina coladas on a purple beach somewhere in the uncharted quadrant. "How about two days off a week to run your own grooming business and you only use flea powder as a secretary when it is necessary?"

Sally crossed her arms and thought for a moment. She could work with that.

"Deal." Then she abruptly turned and started walking towards the door, a stream of toilet paper trailing behind her. "Oh, and someone calling himself a shitter has called three times. You might want to check your voicecomm every once in a while."

Schitter. Brick slammed his drink, then slammed Ivy's second, untouched one that he felt she'd left for him and yelled at Ernie to put it on his tab as raced out to catch up with Sally. He'd call Schitter back from his flat.

They both climbed into his starvette. Brick briefly wondered how Sally had gotten to the bar, then decided he didn't care. Brick hit the autopilot for home. He stretched back and closed his eyes for a sobering nap.

31 ARE YOU TALKING TO YOURSELF?

Back in his apartment, Brick sat waiting on Jagger. He thought about his conversation with Schitter. The half man was certifiably insane. No matter how many times Schitter reassured him it was all perfectly legal, well at least Brick's part in it, an uneasy tension had settled in his stomach along with a nagging sense of, *what the vortexed hell have I gotten into?*

He kept glancing at the ceiling, certain the Tax Authority would collapse through it at any moment and start assaulting themselves until Brick told them something. Then again, he didn't really know anything valuable he hadn't already told Ivy. Then another again, having all the information had never stopped the Tax Authority agents from injuring themselves before. They were a ruthless unit. Brick shivered.

What was taking Jagger so long? He was supposed to be back with Elona, already. Schitter had been explicit about bringing her along so she could see her dad delivered safe and sound for herself. He had a feeling Elona would not be nearly as impressed with the pirate's plan as Schitter seemed to think. But, that was a family problem. He wasn't paid to sort out daddy issues. Still, the whole thing seemed wrong.

Maybe he could be a real hero? What if he used his position to capture the elusive Schitter and rescue Hilep and save the Head of UGH in the mix? He could do it. The plan began unfolding in his brain, charting out a path of success so easy to follow it felt a crime to ignore.

Bam!

"Oh, shit I forgot I used to leave that there."

Brick turned and faced himself, or rather, a very haggard version of himself.

"Uhhhh…"

"Good choice of words. I just managed to sneak out for a few, so I don't have much time before Being Resources crashes through a window."

"The window?"

"Yeah, appears the Tax authority has sole access to ceilings."

Brick nodded to himself. He looked pale, like he hadn't seen daylight in years.

His second self looked around. "Good," he muttered. "I think I got it right." He looked at himself. "I stole a couch to get here. Don't do it. Just don't. Don't."

"Don't do what?"

"That idea you have, saving Hilep, the Head and tossing Schitter in jail. Don't."

"Why? It would be so easy."

Brick laughed, a maniacal, wild laugh. The kind of laugh that ensures everyone knows exactly how crazy and unstable he could be. "Just don't. Trust me, follow the plan and everyone gets what they deserve."

"Do I get paid?"

"Uh, I don't rightfully know. I just know you don't want to be where I have spent the last five years. Trust me, you want Schitter locked up?"

"I really don't care about that. I just thought Ivy..."

"Won't work. Might've worked if it hadn't been for that last bit. But no way around that. Just listen, you are no criminal mastermind."

Brick really was not sure what he meant by telling himself that. He felt inexplicably drawn to the plan inside his head and wondered if this was another anti-paradoxical event defining his life.

A thud at the window caught his attention.

"I've got to go. Listen. Don't do it. Just don't."

MARQ TRUONG

32 PICKLESNOT

B rick watched himself run out of the room and heard the door zip open and close. He thought about all the times he'd taken a couch back to try and fix that one assignment gone awry and wondered if there was some kind of temporal affect which prevented him from giving himself a defined explanation of what goes wrong, why and how to change it. His own warnings were always so generic. The best he got out of himself was that it might have worked except for that bit at the end, but what was that bit? If he could just change that bit, then maybe there would be a better outcome. Of course, how would he know if he were really changing that bit or not, or if how he changes that bit was exactly what he shouldn't have done and that ended up being the bad last bit?

Brick rubbed his temples. Paradoxes gave him a headache. He heard the door swish open. Jagger.

Finally. He was a hyperintelligent being. Maybe he could sort it out. Either way, they needed a solid plan. And he had one. A good one. But, Brick did not want to end up in prison, cryostasis, or wherever the him that just left had been for five years.

33 CHECK, PLEASE!

Elona slumped into the room. "So, have you worked out how to get my dad home yet?" She dropped into a chair, crossed her arms and frowned at him.

To hell with it, Brick thought. "I have an idea," he said and smiled.

MARQ TRUONG

34 I DIDN'T ORDER THAT

Brick had two hours before the meeting time as he slipped carefully into the domiciles of St. Joseph's Blessed Racing Pits.

His last encounter there had been less than pleasant. Granted, there was absolutely nothing pleasant about the domiciles at St. Joseph's. The Yogalarians in charge still held a grudge against him, demanding repayment for Brick winning a bet he should have lost. He'd been captured, locked in a room and subjected to the Dorvanian Torture Technique[25]. The detective had barely survived with his sanity intact and he'd never recovered his stolen sock.

---

[25] **Dorvanian Torture technique:** *Developed by the Kulus Tribe and named after their most infamous leader, Dorvan. The Kulus would capture rival tribe members and submit them to heinous torture, placing them in tents with mediocre lighting, uncomfortable furnishings, stale food and bad beverages until they succumbed to boredom so complete, they would do or say anything to break the monotony.*

He pushed back the gag reflex which sought to overwhelm him from the odor as it slammed against his nostrils. The smell was worse than he recalled. He needed to move quickly up into the kitchens. Brick could ill afford to become distracted by things like smells, large piles of garbage or the green moss creeping along the floor next to the bathroom. The lower level, employee dormitories were infamous for their atrocious living conditions. There were rumors it even housed a glebulor succor worm, but Brick doubted it. The creatures ate garbage. The place would be a lot cleaner, even if it wouldn't smell better.

He squelched across the slimy floor making his way to the lift at the end of the hall. He just had to ignore everything. That was the trick. Ignore the sticky floor, the brown ooze dripping from the ceiling that looked suspiciously like a sewage leak, the pungent odor, and the roaches skittering across the walls.

Finally, he made it to the lift and stepped inside. So far, so good, he hadn't been discovered or chased. Although, Brick conceded, he might have gotten through the dormitories much faster had there been something chasing him. He cleaned off his shoes on the mat provided, which he found quite considerate, considering.

35 TOADSTOOL SALAD, CUT THE TOAD

The lift opened up at the back of the kitchens. Brick heard a great deal of hustle nearby. Brick knew from experience he just needed to ignore them all and act like he belonged there, like he knew where he was going and why. Of course, he wasn't entirely sure where he was going or why he was bothering. There was still no contract obligating anyone to pay him anything. He had warned himself not to do this and now it was affecting his concentration.

He was spotted almost immediately once he stepped away from the lift.

"Hey! Mister! Hold up! What are you doing here?"

Great. His heart just wasn't into ignoring everything. Now what? Brick contemplated what to tell the man. He looked pretty normal. Just a guy in a white apron stained with what looked like gravy, a bit overweight and altogether just a bit too sweaty to be handling food, but otherwise, a nice enough seeming fellow. So, Brick settled on the truth. He figured it would probably work as well as a lie, especially since he couldn't think of one at the moment.

"Well, chap, I just managed to sneak through the domicile level to make it up here, where I suspect one of the politician closets is housing Hilep against his will. I'm also betting the Yogalarians do not know Hilep is here. They have full licensing for the detention and restraint of politicians, but not for the kidnap, restraint, and holding of private citizens, no matter how wealthy they are. Also, they make a good chunk of money off of Hilep and have probably noticed a slump in their profits over the last few days he's been missing."

The man looked at Brick, took off his chef hat and scratched his head. He leaned close. "Hilep tips well. We like him." He looked around for anyone paying attention.

No one was. In fact, they appeared to be pointedly ignoring both Brick and the chef.

"I can take you to the hall of closets, just, if you go inside, make sure the door stays open. They only open from the outside. Otherwise you will get stuck."

Brick nodded. "Thanks." Maybe that was the bit he needed to change. Maybe his other self got locked in the politician closet. That would make sense.

He followed the portly man through the kitchen and down a short corridor then stopped at an intersection.

The cook pointed to the left. "Don't go that way," he said and raised his eyebrows pointedly.

Brick nodded and started right.

A hand grabbed his arm, "Where are you going?"

"You said not to go that way, so I'm going this way."

"No. I work here and you clearly don't, so I'm not really supposed to help you. I'm supposed to send you to your demise, but then Hilep would stay locked up, the Tax Authority would bust us up and close us down and I'd be out tips and a job. But if I help you, I could get fired, too. So I'm going to not help you, if you understand."

"No, I really don't."

"It's a hint."

"Oh, so, I should go that way?"

The man nodded his head yes and said, "No."

Brick hated it when amateurs tried to be sneaky. He took a hesitant step towards the left hallway.

The employee nodded vigorously and said, "No. Not that way."

Brick gave him a clap on the shoulder and started down the hall. When he came to the first door he looked back, but the man was gone. *Guess I just have to try them all until I find him.*

.

MARQ TRUONG

36 TOO MUCH BABY SHIT GREEN

He opened the next door and looked inside. Just an old man in a baby shit green suit with a red tie. He deserved being locked up, Brick thought, and closed the door with a snap. He opened another door with no luck, then another, and another, and another.

Three hundred seventy-two doors later Brick found Hilep sitting up, asleep in a metal chair in the center of a dark room. Relieved, he started inside, almost forgetting the sneaky employee's warning. He turned back and slipped his hand in the doorway to prevent it closing. Hilep was too far away to reach and hold the door.

"Psst. Hey, Hilep. Psst. Wake up."

He stubbornly did not wake. Brick wondered if he'd been drugged. That would definitely complicate matters. Nothing for it, he would have to go inside. So, he took off his right shoe and put it in the door jam.

He walked over and nudged the man. It was definitely Hilep, though he looked like he'd lost a bit of weight. His clothes were a touch baggy on him, though they still looked clean and fresh.

"Hey, Hilep. Wake up."

The man started from his sleep. "What? Where?" He blinked several times. "Brick? What are you doing here?"

"I'm rescuing you, of course. Come on, let's get you out of here."

Hilep slowly stood.

"Are you okay?" Brick asked him.

Hilep shook his head, clearing the drowsiness. "Yes, I was just attempting a deep sleep stasis. This is a politician closet. They usually are only opened every few years."

"Well, let's get you upstairs. Your daughter is having a right fit over all this."

"My daughter? Elona is here? You brought my daughter here?"

"Technically, no, I didn't. Jagger did. But it was all part of the arrangement and if she doesn't show up, then she won't be able to distract Schitter long enough for me to get you out and the UGH Agents in to arrest him."

"Schitter?"

"Yes, you know, he kidnapped you. I'm just glad you were able to get a message out to me."

"Wait, what? I didn't message anyone. I've been in a Politician closet. Look around, do you see any way for me to send a message?"

132

Brick obliged and scanned the room. He was right. There was nothing in there except Hilep and the metal chair. That was weird. If not Hilep, then who? But there wasn't time for that. They had to get upstairs.

Brick's voicecomm chirped. He looked at it and answered.

"Jagger. I got him."

"Well hurry your lazy ass up. It's getting extremely uncomfortable up here."

"Seriously? Everything okay? Did Schitter show?"

"Oh yeah, and Elona has been screaming at him for the last twenty minutes. I don't think she's even taken a breath."

"I'm on my way up now."

"Hey! What are you doing here?" A deep voice yelled from down the hallway.

Yogalarians.

"I've got to go. Keep Schitter there, we are on our way. Tell Ivy to be ready."

"Got it."

MARQ TRUONG

37 GOT IT!

Brick stuffed his voicecomm in his pocket and noticed he somehow had a glass of scotch in his hand. *That's timely.* So, he downed it and they took off, Hilep a bit slow on the start.

"Ouch! Shit. Damn it! Damn it. Damnit." Brick yelled as he stumped his toe. He had forgotten his shoe. His hopping on one foot gave Hilep a few seconds to catch up.

"Why are you wearing one shoe? Is that a new style? How long have I been in there?"

"Gadzeil that hurts. No it's not. I used my shoe to jam the door. Now go."

Brick heard the footsteps gaining on them, but they just needed to make it to the gold carpet. He could see it ahead. Once he got Hilep to that carpet, he would be a customer, not a prisoner. Yogalarians were ruthless but they did have their rules. Well, unless you owed them money, but Brick felt confident Hilep didn't owe money to anyone. He, on the other hand, couldn't afford to be caught until he could establish Diplomatic Immunity under the protection of an UGH Operation.

He needed Ivy.

Ten steps away. He could hear more feet pounding the floor behind them. Either their pursuers had multiplied, or their pursuer had multiplied his feet.

Five steps.

"I said stop!" He heard the someone yell.

Two steps.

They made it, but Brick kept running.

"For crying out loud, we are on the gold carpet. Why are we still running?"

"Because you might be safe but I'm not."

Hilep panted. He kept himself in decent shape, but still, when you are the wealthiest being in the known universes, you don't tend to do a lot of running. You can pay other people to run for you. "So you owe them money, I take it?"

"Good call."

"How much?"

"I don't really know, they tack on interest, probably a hundred thousand viduries by now."

"I'm running over a hundred thousand viduries?" Hilep stopped.

"Come on, we need to get there."

Hilep turned back and faced the pursuer. Turned out it was still just the one and he had six legs.

Brick slowed to a stop while he watched Hilep converse, then he gave a digital signature. The man walked off and Hilep strolled back to meet him.

"Now, can we carry on with just a brisk walk, maybe? I've been in a closet for how long?"

"Four days I think, there abouts."

He nodded. "So, I've been locked in a closet four days,"

"-or there abouts."

"Or there abouts. Point is, I'm a bit winded."

"Did you pay my debt?" Brick blurted.

"Yes."

"Uh..."

"Don't thank me." Hilep waved his hand, dismissing the idea of gratitude. "I think it is the going rate for a high profile kidnapping rescue. Plus, it was worth every penny to desist with the running."

"Okay." It wasn't really the payday Brick was looking for, but not having Yoglarians on his tail constantly would be a good thing. Add the reward for Schitter and jackpot. He might could afford two bathrooms so he didn't have to share with Jagger. What that creature did to a bathroom was just disgusting. He also needed a new toilet paper dispenser.

38 IT'S SHOW TIME!

They turned into the antechamber, from where all the private party boxes were accessed. It looked the same as it had the last time he saw it. It had way too much gilded furniture, too many naked people pretending to be statues, and statues pretending to be naked people.

He saw Ivy and made directly for her.

"Gadzeil, Brick. Took you long enough."

He sighed. "Yes, well, I didn't get to saunter in through the front door and just wait around impatiently, where is everyone?

She turned and looked at the gold door with Hilep's name engraved above it. "In there. Shall we?" She looked down the hall, "Come on boys. Show time."

"I'm surprised you didn't bring the Tax Authority, they've been hunting this guy for years."

"Oh, they are ready to drop in if anything goes amiss."

Brick nodded, but looked around as he did so. There was an element missing. "Where is the Head?"

Ivy smiled, and she gave a sly chuckle. "Oh, he's inside. He has no idea you have rescued Hilep."

"Why?"

"Because Schitter is not the only criminal we are bringing down today." She replied.

"I'm not one of them, am I?" Brick asked.

"Not today, Brick." She shook her head then turned and addressed Hilep. "Sir, if you don't mind please waiting just a few moments. We want to secure the felons before you enter, for your own safety and the safety of others."

"Of course, Miss Cee." He gave her a pleasant smile.

"Thank you." She turned back to the door and bade Brick to follow her inside. He was the official liaison, after all.

Before following, Hilep caught Brick's arm and whispered, "I quite like her. You should ask her out."

Brick rolled his eyes then limped after Ivy, the big toe on his right foot throbbing.

"Why are you missing a shoe?" Ivy asked.

"I donated it to a good cause."

39 TWO HALF MEN WALK INTO A BAR...

n the doorway Brick was met with a familiar, angry voice.

"Oh and when I was eight, you missed my ballet recital, my dumbonx pageant, and I played the lead caterpillar, I had my tonsil removed and nothing, nothing from my left dad."

"Eh, hem. Elona? Excuse me, dove, but Brick is here." Ivy cut in, kindly.

Elona turned from her left dad, whose half face that was not android looked ashen. He gave Brick a thankful look, which made Brick feel a twinge of guilt. Or maybe that was just all the drinking on an empty stomach. He needed some food after all of this.

"Oh, good. I was getting tired," Elona said, then walked away and sat in a chair, arms crossed and did a very good job of looking like she hated everyone and everything in the universe.

"Okay agents, please place them under arrest."

There was a large outcry. First from Schitter, then the head, who Brick had just noticed standing there in a crumpled suit, but it was the Being Resources Director of UGH that marched up making demands.

"Excuse me, Miss Cee."

"Call me Ivy, please," she responded with a catty smile.

Brick knew instantly these two did not get along.

"Miss Cee, this is a ransom exchange, as you well know, and a perfectly legal format." She pointed at Schitter, "He has a kidnapped victim of significant universal value and has legally made the request to assume the position of Head at UGH in return for the safe and immediate release of said hostage." She turned to Brick, "I understand Mr. Schitter has named you as his liaison. Are you ready to proceed?"

"Well, about that..." Brick started.

Ivy cut in. "Yes, about that. Mr. Schitter has no hostage to exchange, therefore, there is no negotiation and certainly no immunity from punishment."

"Wait, what? What do you mean there is no hostage?" It was the small man in the crumpled suit, Nutor Guttor. Head of the Ultimate Galactic Headquarters. "How is it there is no one to exchange?" He turned and glared at Schitter. "How the hell did you screw this up? It was so easy."

Schitter looked perplexed. It echoed his own thoughts, really. It had all been easy. Way too easy. It began to feel like a setup from the beginning.

"I'll save you the bother," Ivy interjected. "Brick rescued him while Schitter argued with his daughter."

"I'd hardly call it arguing," one of the agents muttered.

"I don't see him. Where is he? Can you prove he was rescued?" The Head demanded.

"He's right outside." Ivy answered.

"But Mr. Wilson brought him, right?" A sly look crossed Nutor's pointy face.

"Yes," she replied.

"That's close enough. He works for Schitter, so it is the same thing as still being in Schitter's control."

"Uhhhh," Brick said.

"Detective Wilson, do you work for Mr. Schitter?" Asked the Being Resource Director.

"Well, no not really."

"What I mean is, do you have a contract? Did Mr. Schitter place your services for the liaison and delivery of Hilep under contract?"

"Oh, no."

"You didn't put him under contract?" Nutor turned to Schitter, throwing his hands in the air. "What kind of evil genius are you? You were spoon fed the whole thing, but I thought even you wouldn't overlook that part. Gadzeil!"

"Wait, what? Spoon fed? By who?" Then realization struck Schitter. The woman he loved was a farce. "You hired her. None of it was real."

"You are an idiot," Nutor snapped. "I'll never get another chance at it. Damn it."

"Well, that would be correct, Head Guttor. I am afraid your actions are in direct violation of your contract." The Being Resource Director pulled out her morally deplete blaster and shot the Head in the head.

His lifeless form fell to the floor.

She turned her blaster on Schitter. "Agents, please place Mr. Schitter under arrest. And please see that Head Guttor is returned to the office so we can prop him up for his early retirement party."

The men moved into action.

"Could you call in Hilep, please, Miss Cee?"

"Of course, Matilda," she answered.

Matilda? Brick did not think she looked like a Matilda at all. He'd known a few, even dated one, obviously not this Matilda. This Matilda did not look like the kind of being who dated anyone, especially with the morally deplete blaster still smoking in her hand and the Head of UGH dead on the floor.

Ivy ushered Hilep into the room. Elona ran over and hugged him, to which he seemed genuinely surprised.

Brick thought maybe things would work out okay after all. Given he got paid by someone.

"Hilep," Matilda started, "Did this man, Brick Wilson, in fact rescue you and bring you here?"

"Oh, yes. He found me in a politician closet on these premises."

"Thank you." She turned to Brick. "Head Nutor Guttor was in violation of his contract and subject to the terms of immediate early retirement. Schitter was unable to complete the transaction necessary to gain the Head's position. You, however, delivered the victim within your sole custody and released him. Since the position must be filled, I have deemed you qualified and would, with your consent, name you the next Head of UGH from this day forward until such time as a new Head of UGH is appointed or your retirement. Will you agree?"

Head of UGH? Brick's brain reeled at the possibility. He looked around the room. It could fix so many things. He saw Jagger in his trench coat trying to avoid being noticed. He could grant Jagger immunity and citizenship. He saw Ivy, the only real woman he had ever, well, the only real woman he'd ever considered worth putting a toilet seat down for. Granted, he had never considered putting the toilet seat down for any fake women, either. Still, there was one question which needed answering, first, before all the good deed and maybe reconnecting with his ex stuff. "What does it pay?"

Matilda smiled. They always asked that. Everything else was bait, but this was the hook. "An untold fortune."

"Untold fortune? How much is that?"

"If I told you, then it wouldn't be untold. Let's just say it is more than enough."

"More than enough for what?"

"Anything you have the time and will to spend it on."

It sounded good. Too good. He looked down, thinking. Suddenly, Matilda's shoes turned bright Red.

Brick grimaced. Then smiled. He could outlaw Red completely. He clapped his hands together. That did sound good. "Okay. Let's do it."

"Brick," Ivy began, "you may want to think about it."

"Now, dear, he already knows what he wants. He's already said yes." Matilda chimed, happily.

With that, Brick Wilson became the 2,379,427th Head of the Ultimate Galactic Universe.

The door busted open and in walked Sally cradling two toilet paper dispensers. Brick wondered if the one multiplied or had she liberated a second one to keep the first one company.

"There you are! I've been looking for you."

"Uh, Sally. Not a good time, could you wait outside?" Brick replied.

She looked at him. "Not you."

She walked by Brick and sauntered up to Schitter.

"You. I've been looking for you."

"Me? Who are you?" Schitter asked.

"Not you." She glared at his left eye. "You," she said and looked deep into his right, android eye.

"Well, that clears everything up," Brick started.

Then Sally kissed Schitter. A long, passionate kiss. Long enough to make everyone else very uncomfortable, including Schitter, who was handcuffed.

Sally finally pulled away, smiled and walked out of the room, everyone watching, perplexed, as she went.

Happy ending, right?

40 ELSEWHERE INSIDE HALF AN ANDROID

Vinny stretched and looked around. He could not sense any activated personality drives.

Interesting. He walked along the wall that appeared to fuse humanoid and android. That could prove a definite challenge, but it certainly intrigued his mischievous programming. He pressed his hand against a cold diode.

"This will be fun," he muttered and dove into the circuitry in search of disabled personality protocols. Whatever fool had attached himself to an android was in for a big surprise.

31 AGAIN
ARE YOU LISTENING TO YOURSELF?
(SEVERAL HOURS EARLIER)

B ack in his apartment, Brick sat waiting on Jagger. He thought about his conversation with Schitter. The half man was certifiably insane. No matter how many times Schitter reassured him it was all perfectly legal, well at least Brick's part in it, an uneasy tension had settled in his stomach along with a nagging sense of, *what the vortexed hell have I gotten into?*

He kept glancing at the ceiling, certain the Tax Authority would collapse through it at any moment and start assaulting themselves until Brick told them something. Then again, he didn't really know anything valuable he hadn't already told Ivy. Then another again, having all the information had never stopped the Tax Authority agents from injuring themselves before. They were a ruthless unit. Brick shivered.

What was taking Jagger so long? He was supposed to be back with Elona, already. Schitter had been explicit about bringing her along so she could see her dad delivered safe and sound for herself. He had a feeling Elona would not be nearly as impressed with the pirate's plan as Schitter seemed to think. But, that was a family problem. He wasn't paid to sort out daddy issues. Still, the whole thing seemed wrong.

Maybe he could be a real hero? What if he used his position to capture the elusive Schitter and rescue Hilep and save the Head of UGH in the mix? He could do it. The plan began unfolding in his brain, charting out a path of success so easy to follow, it felt a crime to ignore.

Bam!

"Oh, shit I forgot I used to leave that there."

Brick turned and faced himself, or rather, a very haggard version of himself.

"Uhhhh..."

"Good choice of words. I just managed to sneak out for a few, so I don't have much time before Being Resources crashes through a window."

"A window?"

"Yeah, appears the Tax authority has sole access to ceilings."

Brick nodded to himself. He looked pale, like he hadn't seen daylight in years.

"Good. I stole a couch to get here. Don't do it. Just don't. Don't."

"Don't do what?"

"That idea you have, saving Hilep, the Head and tossing Schitter in jail. Don't."

"Why? It would be so easy."

Bam! Flump!

"Shit! Gadzeil! Who left that there?" Came Brick's voice. Another Brick limped into the room and stood next to the other future self.

"What the hell? How many of you are there? Or me, rather?"

"Two too many in this room, said the first extra Brick."

"No time. Being Resources, remember?"

"Quite right."

"Okay," the second future Brick looked at the not future Brick, "Don't do it. For the love of anything, or the hate of anything, or whatever the vortexed hell that will motivate you to nix the hero fever you are feeling right now. Do you want to end up hiding in a closet for the next five years? Well, I can tell you, you don't."

"True that," the first future Brick chimed in.

"Just make the exchange, no funny crap, no saving anyone because no one is coming to save you."

At that moment the window crashed open. In climbed a very smart looking businesswoman in a baby shit green suit. Her name tag identified her as Matilda, UGH Director of Being Resources. She held a blaster up and instantly shot the second future Brick while the first one ran for it. She strolled into the hallway and blasted the first future Brick just as he reached the door. Lowering her morally deplete early retirement/termination blaster, she walked back in the room. Brick had not moved from his seat. He looked up from his own dead form to her, wondering what was about to happen. She seemed contemplating whether or not to shoot him as well, but without a word, she shrugged and jumped out the window.

Brick's gaze returned to his own dead image on the floor. Not bloody cool at all. He could feel his heart pounding. The swish of the door and subsequent screaming announced the arrival of Jagger and Elona.

41 ANTI-PARIDOXICAL EVENT SAY WHAT?
(STILL SEVERAL HOURS EARLIER THAN BEFORE)

"It's okay," Brick yelled. "I'm in here."

Jagger came bounding in and found another dead Brick and a very much alive Brick sitting in a chair, if not a bit pale.

"Was this your plan? Suicide?"

"This is seriously messed up," Elona said as she walked in to discover the rest of the scene.

"No, I don't think it was suicide. I think it is an elaborate message."

"From whom?" Jagger asked. "Is it a threat?"

"No. It's a warning. From me."

"A warning? Well, that's good. You said you had a plan and I'm betting we need all the help we can get."

"Yeah, Jagger said you have a plan to get my dad back."

"Right. A plan. The plan." He leaned forward and tapped his pinky on the coffee table. It made a wonderfully soothing clicking noise. *The plan.*

"Nope. I have no plan."

"What? What do you mean, no plan? You are just going to give my left dad what he wants?"

Brick looked back at his own, haggard body on the floor. "Yes. That is exactly what we are going to do."

"But," Elona began.

Brick quickly interrupted her.

"But nothing. We are going to give Schitter exactly what he is asking for. Something," he looked pointedly down to his own limp body, then back at Elona, "something tells me it is not the same thing as getting what he wants."

He stood up. "Let's get this over with. If I'm right, then there won't be any bodies to incinerate when we are done, which would be good because I don't want to pay for my own funeral twice before I die."

42 BLUE

With a pop, Brick's starvette turned from baby shit green to bluer than blue blue. All across the universe baby shit green winked out and was replaced with beautiful shades of bright, soft, muted and even shadowy blues. Baby shit green retreated to the interior contents of used diapers. Suddenly the universe smelled much more pleasant. Except for the used diapers. Those still smelled off.

Just like that, Blue returned from his vacation, unannounced. It hadn't been all that amazing. Everywhere he tried to go and relax, baby shit green, a distant sixth cousin three times removed, showed up. He'd spent most of his existence ignoring the color. Baby Shit was the type that showed up to family reunions always pretending to be more important than the reality of his life. He'd had a very brief moment of popularity when some designers thought to give him a try, but it only lasted one embarrassing season before the fashion police arrested those responsible. No, working was preferable to listening to the pretender gleefully whine and complain about the high demand of his presence, and Blue was not a fan of shit green oceans and skies. He just couldn't relax. Blue eased comfortably into place, still pissed off at Red, but happy the nasty smell was dissipating.

Red popped up on the tail pipes.

"Get the fuck away from me."

"I'm not touching you!"

"Don't make me call mom."

"You are no fun at all." And Red winked out.

Vigradian Appendix

Vigradian Appendix: An appendix method utilizing the Vigradian Alphabet.

Vigradian Alphabet: A twenty-five lettered alphabet developed on the planet Cob. However, the name Cob Alphabet or Cobian Alphabet did not sound pleasant, so it was renamed Vigradian so as to appeal to a greater number of beings in the Universe. This alphabet has been adopted and utilized by both the Calssificationist Guild and the Ultimate Galactic Dictionary. The order is thus: V K P Z T I (except on Tuesdays, where the I comes before the T, making it rather important to know what day of the week it is) L U S G A C F W O Y R Q E N B J D H M. The Vigradian alphabet does not recognize X as a letter and maintains that it is just a KS, and sometimes a Z, sound posing as a letter. Therefore anything spelled with an X is automatically alphabetized as KS or Z, respectively.

Vidurie(s): The primary monetary resource in the Ultimate Galactic Universe, accepted as recompense in most business transactions, including those for merchandise, services and payment of Ultimate Galactic Headquarters Taxes, Surcharges and Fines. The Vidurie is backed by the UGH Galactic Bank's stockpile of Ptyridactoplatimus scales.

Vadurian Standard Time: All commerce, taxes and subjugate fines in the Ultimate Galactic Universe are based on the Standard Vadurian time. Since the only time constant in the universe is measured in seconds, and there are so ridiculously many seconds to account for in the four tenses of the universe, and while individual planets, solar systems and sectors may have adopted unique denotations for the passage of time (hours, minutes, days, months, years), the legal considerations of time are Based on the Vadurian Equation.

v=Vadurian, s=second(s), m=minute(s), h=hour(s), d=day(s), mm=month(s), y=year(s), c=constant

1sc=1sv

48sv=1mv

160mv=1hv

12hv=1dv

.25dv=1mmv

3mmv=1yv

Through this given equation, any time equivalent in the Ultimate Universe can be configured to the Vadurian Standard.

Kultren IV: The planet know as Kultren is actually Kultren IV, although there are not three previous Kultrens. It is a small planet in Quadrant XVII which orbits the crimson sun, Jolton. It boasts twenty-five percent landmass and seventy-five percent fresh water ocean. The sky is normally a bluish purple due to ions in the atmosphere. There are two, large, triangular shaped continents, inhabited by the Reen'os, a feline civilization. Kutren IV is circled by two uninhabited moons, Ceket and Leero. It is considered a TAL 5. It was discovered by the future Star Prophet Woodrow White after falling asleep on a couch watching videos in about a thousand year post hence.

Pzyboribean Flatnut: Approximately thirty-five centimeters in length, thirty centimeters in height and about twenty centimeters at its center, the thickest point. Brownish-green with bright orange marbling across the surface. Found on the grey, sandy shores of Pzyboribea IV. Despite hundreds of years of arguments between scientists and classificationists, it is still unclear as to whether the now infamous Pzyboribean Flatnut is actually a nut or a shellfish. Each experimental research period to resolve the question has received exorbitant funding by the Ultimate Galactic Headquarters, but yielded identical, exasperating results. Repeated testing has shown that upon opening a Pzyboribean Flatnut, one will always find a very happy, sleepy and fat Clobit Worm inside. This frustrates the scientists, who insist the Clobit Worm is not indigenous to Pzyboribea IV, but traditionally found in the jungles of Wallupta, located in Quadrant IX, whereby Pzyboribea IV is found in the not neighboring Quadrant VIII. Recently interjecting themselves into the mix are the Theoreticists who postulate that the Clobit Worms believe Quadrant IX should neighbor Quadrant VIII, and therefore, because they believe so, it does. The Scientists argue that this still does not explain how the Clobit Worm got from Quadrant VIII to Quadrant IX, no matter where in the Ultimate Universe it is located. The Classificationists say that neither matter, because the Clobit Worm is not a seed, so the Pzyboribean Flatnut is therefore, not a nut, also noting that the shell is, in fact, not flat. Therefore, since the Pzyboribean Flatnut, is not a nut, nor is it flat and is apparently not even from Pzyboribea IV, then it does not exist at all, whereby making all arguments over it moot, and to call them when someone has some actual evidence that it exists.

Ptyridactoplatimus: The scientific name for a small, extinct species of reptimarmovarian. Actually, the only known species of reptimarmovarian to ever exist in nature. A reptimarmovarian is a genetic mutation crossing a reptile, a mammal, a marsupial and a bird. While this is not uncommon in illegal genetic laboratories, the Ptyridactoplatimus somehow evolved of its own accord and promptly died out, spawning a whole new field of archaeology before a whole new field of biology could emerge. But since there was only one species, the field remained quite small and there are only three known Reptimarmoviologists remaining in the Ultimate Galaxy, all otherwise and elsewhere employed. The Ptyridactoplatimus is a small, winged, scaled creature with a beak, a pouch and a spiked tail. It was flightless, hopping on its back legs and theoretically using its small wings to balance itself as it hopped. The Ptyridactoplatimus reproduced by laying eggs, which would instantly hatch and the young climb into the pouch. The species was revered for its colorful scales and its extinction is given credit for the destruction of the planet once called Plaid, though only a very few in the galaxy would make the connection as the creature is more commonly known as the Pesnort, due to the odd sound it supposedly made and the fact that Pesnort is comparatively much easier to say than Ptyridactoplatimus. See Pesnort for more information. *On a further note, for the sake of full disclosure and to prevent any lawsuits, the Conservatory of Ultimate Galactic Classificationists, also known as the Classificationist Guild, state they were never contacted to determine how to properly classify the Ptyridactoplatimus, and since it does not fit in any accepted category previously established, as they do not recognize the classification of reptimarmovarian because they did not create it and they claim names and categories clearly fall into their jurisdiction, the Ptyridactoplatimus, therefore, does not exist until such time as they receive a formal work order and proper funding to commence with said work order. See Pesnort.

Plaid: Not the most exciting name for a planet, but its former inhabitants were not very exciting. Presently, the planet formerly known as Plaid, houses Dave's Drive-thru Donut Planet. Before it was a donut planet, it was primarily rubble. Before it was primarily rubble, it was a lush, green planet filled with life. Not the brightest life, but still life. It was Plaid. On Plaid, evolution seemed to be a bit unsure of itself, going one direction and changing its mind, scrapping the idea and starting something new. Evolution had done a lot of really spectacular things elsewhere and was running out of ideas to top itself. As a result, a species had little time to evolve before Evolution decided it wasn't working out and sent a plague to wipe the fledgling life into extinction. Eventually, Evolution just gave up when it saw some monkeys somewhere else it could play with and ran off. This left Plaid to its own devices with what Evolution had left behind.

Plaid was inhabited by many creatures. The most intelligent and dominant were the Plaidlet race. This race went into near extinction after a scientist visited the planet and made the mistake of using the term, "survival of the fittest." The Plaidlets took this as wise words from a prophet of the stars and determined only the strongest should be allowed to survive. Thus they developed the custom of dropping newborn Plaidlets in the great river and waiting downstream to pull them out again. If the infant survived, then it was deemed, "fit to live." This created a rather gruesome infant mortality rate and intergalactic conservationists insisted that new star prophets be sent to correct the dilemma. After many arguments, the Plaidlets changed their practices, deciding to throw the star prophets in the river and wait downstream. If they survived, then they were determined "fit to live." This was seen as a significant advancement in sociological behavior and deductive reasoning.

Evolution heard about it and was considering making another trip around that way, but was distracted by some phosphorescent plankton in Quadrant XXXVII.

A Star Prophet noticed another species on the planet, a beautiful reptilian, birdlike, mammal like, marsupial like creature covered in beautiful scales which caught the light and glimmered as individual jewels encrusting its body. However, he was promptly thrown in the river and drowned, so the animal's discovery was delayed another hundred years, after the Plaidlets were getting a little tired of throwing Star Prophets in the river. It had become all too popular to adventure seekers wanting to claim the title of "Fit to Live" for themselves. The Plaidlets were becoming disgruntled with all the stupid requests of the star prophets as well, like eating breakfast standing on your head and knocking a coconut against a stone three times before taking a wee. However, all of this changed when an entrepreneur Star Prophet selling "Fit to Live" t-shirts at the end of the river rapids spotted a Pesnort sitting on a small stone watching nothing in particular. He asked a local about the creature, who told him they were good to bar-b-que. He approached the docile animal, which jumped in fright and slowly, haphazardly, hopped away, flapping its tiny wings and leaving a trail of scales behind. This moment is credited with the demise of Plaid.

The jewel-like scales became all the rage. Wealthy people all across the galaxy wanted the scales for anything and everything, willing to pay ridiculous sums to acquire them. The star prophet wanted to keep the viduries for himself, but upon hearing this, the Plaidlets felt he should be tried as a star prophet again and was subsequently thrown back in the river, several times, until he wore so many fit to live t-shirts that they weighed him down and he disappeared beneath the raging rapids never to be seen again. After this, the Plaidlets were overwhelmed with sudden wealth. Since Evolution had abandoned them, they would buy what could not be given by millions of years of trial and error. Planets, solar systems and entire galaxies, up to and including the Ultimate Galactic Headquarters, just starting up in a smallish way at that time and largely unknown, sought to acquire the scales for themselves, stockpiling any they could get hold of. The Plaidlets quickly tired of the Viduries, as they tried eating them, wearing them and throwing them at one another with only minimal success. Someone, who remains unnamed as he does not like being attributed with the second moment which brought about the destruction of Plaid, came up with the idea of helping these people out with some technology to make their lives easier in exchange for the priceless scales. His idea took on rather well, since there was much technology in the universe to be had and it would cost virtually no viduries to give it to the Plaidlets. So, the Plaidlets became supplied with ever-increasingly advanced technologies, most of which they did not understand, so they traded more Pesnort scales for people who did understand and could explain it. When they could not understand the explanations, they traded yet more scales for people who could just use the technology for them and let them get on with bar-b-queing the Pesnorts, as to have more scales in which to buy more things they did not know how to use. After a very few Vadurian years, the planet of Plaid had been transformed into a high tech metropolis of sky-rise buildings housing all the people who worked there. A small section of jungle had been quartered off for the Plaidlets who did not understand things like doors, toilets or the postal system, and preferred living in the trees. However they enjoyed their success and determined to prove they could make progress of their own accord and being so determined, they additionally determined they would have a holiday celebration. They decided to celebrate the Pesnort, which had brought them so much glorious fortune. To celebrate, they gathered all the Pesnorts together and had a huge Bar-b-que in their honor. The Pesnorts did not feel very honored, as they were what was being bar-b-qued. After the three day feast, they began paying off the bills with the scales they'd collected. But as the entire species had been eaten, the reserves of Pesnort scales ran low. There was a rush to get paid once the public learned of the sudden extinction of the creature. People began packing up and leaving Plaid in droves as the economy took a sharp dive. The value of scales went up and the wealthy became wealthier, selling off their scales for huge profits. Meanwhile, the Plaidlets were left alone and hungry in a tiny section of the jungle. Determined not to be the fools of the universe, they ventured into the metropolis. They would learn to use the technology left behind, wondering how hard it could be. Red buttons winked at them everywhere, which looked like good places to start, so they hit them all at once and the planet blew up, leaving a huge hole through the center and shearing away vast portions of its mantle as well. The atmosphere disintegrated, and a collective, "oops" floated through space.

In an alternate time parody occupying the same space and universe, almost ten thousands highly evolved Pesnorts spontaneously fell into the giant bar-b-que pit during the great feast. As a result, the Plaidlets had food and scales for a little longer than they otherwise would have had before they ventured into the Metropolis and subsequently blew themselves to smithereens.

Plaidlet: The indigenous, humanoid population which once occupied the Planet Plaid.

Psycho Waste Collection and Disposal Unit: a tool used by the Psycho Waste Department, a privately owned, taxpayer supported sub-branch of the Ultimate Galactic Headquarters. The Collection and Disposal Units were the invention of a little known Psycho-Scientist named, well no one knows his name, and in effect, even if it were known, writing it here would be oxymoronic for it would no longer be little known. Stating the psycho-scientist is little known is assuming that the scientist, at least, knows who he or she is, and since this inventor has not come forward, it is assumed that they wish to remain little known and it is therefore the responsibility of this publication to not interfere with the obscure status of the little known psycho-scientist who invented the Psycho Waste Collection and Disposal Unit. The unit, itself, was invented to help reduce traffic and trash in the intergalactic spaceways throughout the Ultimate Galactic Universe. The units are equipped with micro wormhole teleportation and hyperspace drives, rubbish homing devices and psychic-kinetic evaluation modes to ensure the units know where the trash will be before it is discarded. They are then set to a specific regional signature to collect garbage. Once the container is full, utilizing the micro wormhole technology, it opens a rift in space, teleporting it to an aligned disposal location, where it relieves itself of its contents and instantly returns to its beat to collect more rubbish. The Psycho Waste Collection and Disposal Units are each designed to fixate on a specific life form, a Giant Glebular Succor Worm, given refuge in remote locations throughout the galaxy. No one wants Giant Glebular Succor Worms near their residential areas because they feast on waste, trash and many other smelly, nasty things no one wants where they live. This makes the Giant Glebular Succor Worm smell rather bad, itself. The worms were quick to strike a deal with the Ultimate Galactic Universe when offered all the free food they could eat and a nice, quiet place to digest it.

Pot: Pot is a small, purplish planet in Quadrant I which mostly consists of water. The indigenous sentient species of the planet, Potheads, has long been extinct, slaughtered at a Pot Party which the inhabitants threw in anticipation of their extinction. The invading Nerelon force, though amphibious, did not wish to share the planet with a bunch of Potheads, afraid they would drive down property values. See also: Potheads, Nerelon, Neros.

Potheads: An extinct, sentient species from the planet Pot, now inhabited by Nerelons. Potheads were an easy going, on the verge of lazy, species of humanoid who enjoyed living a modest life in tune with the nature of their surroundings. While they were in touch with other planets, they never bothered developing space travel. They were, however, famous for their parties and music festivals. Upon discovering a hostile force bent on their destruction orbiting their planet, they felt it was far too late to start developing or building defensive weapons, shields or war machines. It honestly just sounded like a whole lot of work considering they would probably lose anyway. So, instead, they threw a huge extinction party and even invited the enemy Nerelons, just to show there were no hard feelings. The Nerelons took the opportunity and obliterated the entire race.

Phlemighan's Disease: discovered approximately one point six million years ago, though it is believed to have existed much, much longer. It is contracted from eating contaminated fruit. Phlemango is the root disease and is sexually transmitted through certain species of tropical plants. The subsequent fruit of those plants are contaminated with a byproduct called Phlemaghan. Those beings which consume said contaminated fruit have a thirty-two percent chance of contracting Phlemaghan's Disease. The condition attacks speech perception and reactionary functions which cause the individual to talk about pineapples. It is a progressive illness, beginning with random, out of context mentioning of pineapples, then progresses to sentences and conversations which focus entirely on pineapples. In the late stages of the illness, "Pineapple" is all they can say. There is no known cure. The disease was eradicated in the multiverse when a plant friendly sex education program was introduced, encouraging safe pollination practices and reproduction/fruiting control options.

Theory of Relativity: First, the Theory of Relativity is actually the Law of Relativity, but it just doesn't sound as nice to say, so it is still called the Theory of Relativity by most everyone except the diehard Lawologists. Since most people do not care what the Lawologists think, and they receive relatively little funding from the Ultimate Galactic Headquarters, their complaints are largely dismissed and ignored.

The Galactic Guild of Civil Relations and Time Continuity, at its 2,354th Annual conference unanimously agreed upon the Theory of Relativity. Well, almost unanimously, 159 votes of Aye and one vote abstained because he was locked, gagged in a closet. The guild had spent over 2,000 years working on this theory and they were not about to let one old fogey determined to insist time was constant to stand in the way of progress. Since everyone present to vote, voted Aye, the Theory of Relativity was passed into law and now is the dominant resource for determining all factors of time. Some other science branches had to do some quick shifts, as time no longer remaining constant jumbled up their calculations a bit. Time had to do some shifting as well to keep up with progress, but not wanting to be left out of the loop, it has done its job sportingly. Anyway, being constant was terribly boring and jumping around a bit made eternity much more interesting, so Time was happy to comply.

The Law:

Time is directly related to circumstance. More specifically, to an absolute circumstance. Time passes at different rates depending on if a relative is or is not sleeping on your couch, and then is sped or slowed down by the continuing factor of the nature of the relative sleeping on your couch, and the duration in which they continue to sleep there. Also, it determines that couches are the modem for which time changes itself. Professor Morka Milam, Senior Time Continuity Research Director at Walawala Upta University first discovered the inconsistency of time passage when his wife's brother came to visit after losing his job. It was supposed to be for a weekend. Milam had not complained about his weekend seeming longer, only that he had spent it with his lazy brother-in-law. The weekend stretched into a week, which felt like two. Then two weeks which felt like four. Professor Milam was torn between wanting to research the phenomenon and getting the lazy bum off his couch. The latter won out, but he decided to continue his study using proxy families and detailing their experience and utilizing temporal measurement devices. The devices concluded that inside the home, the presence of unwanted family created a time warp which actually stretched time beyond its original bounds, as much as tripling the length of time passage in extreme cases. The results were phenomenal. Noting that time could, in fact, decide to selectively slow itself down, Milam set out to see if the opposite were also true. His new test subjects were first male college students allowing distantly related, very hot, promiscuous cousins (third, fourth and fifth cousins, typically two or three times removed) to sleep on their couch. This was a vast failure for two reasons. First because most of the male college students did not actually have a couch and second because they quickly moved the cousin to their own beds, usually with the college male still in it. Both instances removed the prime factor of the theory, which is, of course, the time fulcrum: The couch.

Not to be deterred, Milam plugged on utilizing various grants and subcontracting work to further his experiments to various corporations until his sudden demise, involving a couch, a time warp and an egg beater, whereby another up and coming Temporal Theoreticist stepped up to take his place, named Lapnil Schnapp. Schnapp found the flaw in the research tests and determined to place visiting relatives the family enjoyed seeing to sleep on the couch. It was initially difficult to locate suitable test subjects, as most people only enjoy seeing their relatives initially and after the first day or two, the anxiety begins to build. Schnapp used this phenomenon to create a test model of time flow, showing the initial increase in time passage, two days feeling like one. However, after the initial increase, time slowed down to the general passage, denoted at point 0. After four days the time began to slow and the final findings found that one week created a net loss of two days on the average lifespan. The findings were published, debated and accepted into theory, where the guild then spent the next two thousand years deliberating the merits of making it law. And then the next several years explaining how this would apply to things like wormholes, watches, and clock radios.

Theoretical Beology: Theoretical ways to study Beology, implying ramifications outside the specific perimeters of being to involve is and the meaning of is, which happens to be such a small pursuit that it did not qualify under the very lenient structures of the Ultimate Galactic Headquarters, to create a category of its own. A classification order was submitted, but there were no subsequent funds to study the query, so the request for Isology was denied. Theoretic Belologists further suppose why and how one is being and deduce that because one must be in a place at any given time and could be in any place at any given time, then everyone is therefore everywhere at all times.

Theory of De-evolution: The theory of de-evolution was promoted by the psycho waste technician Theoreticists, a.k.a. the thinking garbage collectors of the universe.

The theory goes something like this:
If you consider that there are infinite star systems in the Ultimate Universe, and if even one tenth of one percent of these develop intelligent life forms, and of those, if only one tenth of one percent achieve interstellar travel, they aren't sure how many life forms that is but it does equate to a whopping lot of space travel going on. It is also a well-known galactic fact that for some reason, the more evolved a species becomes, the more trash it produces. Some of the younger and bolder psycho techs ventured to just go ahead and redefine the development of advanced intellect as a sign of de-evolution of the species rather than progress. They state that a primitive species lives in harmony with its environment. It utilizes everything and produces virtually zero waste. The more intelligent they become, two things happen: one, they become inherently lazy, creating things like remote controls so they do not have to walk six feet, and second they begin to pile up heaps of garbage. They do not wish to take care of the garbage themselves, so they hire others to move the garbage for them. Which reverts back to instance one, they are lazy.
This began a short lived Re-Evolution campaign, where the psycho tech union asked planets to stop educating their young, in hopes they would become more stupid and less likely to create mounds of trash, thereby making the job of psycho-techs much easier. Some planets were eager to comply, realizing they could use their ill spent funds on education on more important things like custom colored atmospheres. And while the

theory seemed to be proving correct, as there was less garbage to collect, the psycho tech waste collection and disposal union, facing vast layoffs in personnel as garbage collection became a thing of the past, instituted in its stead an inter-galactic Mardi Gras, thus creating enough rubbish to salvage their jobs. They quietly swept the Re-evolution campaign under the chairperson's rug (it is a very big rug *see other things that may be under Psycho Tech Chairman's rug) and refuse to discuss such ludicrous assumptions of de-evolution again. They also passed a galactic law prohibiting psycho techs from forming theories or thinking.

Inhabitants of Sblitterdot: The Inhabitants of Sblitterdot suffer from what most Psychotheorologists call Mass Paranoiac Delusional Entropy. The entire race (of Inhabitants of Sblitterdot, not Psychotheorologists) believed initially that they must look at their feet to ensure they remained firmly affixed to the ground. From this somewhat harmless, if not awkward, mass paranoia, things took a downward spiral. The most celebrated Psychotheorologist, Alberto Bum, put it as such in his highly unread published thesis on his study of the subjects (It remains highly unread as most people in the known universe simply do not care and those whom might have cared can't read it): Their feet must always touch the ground or they will fall off the planet, into the sky and the vast space beyond, where they would certainly die of fright, asphyxiation or hunger. Their feet would only stay firmly planted to the ground so long as they were closely watched. After all, everyone tends to slack off a bit when the boss isn't looking. Since falling off a planet is nothing to slack off about, the Inhabitants of Sblitterdot kept a watchful eye on their feet and made sure they did their job properly. After long generations, a local scientist developed a new theory, believing that they would only fall off the planet if they could see the sky. Being reasonable, the Inhabitants of Sblitterdot shut themselves up in houses and tried to relax a bit. However, when storm season came, a few misfortunate cyclones swept a few unfortunate occupants away along with their houses. Upon facing this setback, the civilization came to the next logical conclusion: They removed their eyes, as this would completely solve the whole problem of seeing the sky once all the much happier inhabitants emerged from the somewhat painless procedure. It would have been painless except the surgeons, wanting to set a good example for the public, all volunteered to go first, and not being able to see, attempted to blind a few ears, noses and throats by mistake. This, as it turns out, is quite painful. However, the scientist did not take into consideration what the sky could see, so once they emerged from their procedures, they were instantly snatched up and redeposited on a neighboring planet. A fabulous and ultra-smooth marketing team saw the money making potential to sell posotronic seeing dogulets to an entire blind race of beings. That lucky, and now disgustingly wealthy, salesman's name was Henry. (See CAKE) Henry also managed to convince the new heralded scientist, Advar Nork, that it would be a violent disruption to their culture if they did not maintain their sightless traditions by continuing to blind all their citizens from birth. He argued, "It only takes one generation and then the whole world will be gone, floating off who knew where. You, who sat on the edge of the frontier and were pushed back to keep from falling off into it, will be forgotten, left to file lawsuits and walk into each other at marches on city halls, just to stop the spoiled, bright eyed brats from kicking you out of the society you sacrificed to give them. They'll have you begging on corners, selling canned pencils." He raged on. It really got to the heart of their fears, prickled something they did not altogether feel very good about being prickled. Though, they did not know what canned pencils were nor why they should sit on corners and sell them, they felt obliged to take matters firmly in hand. They hailed Henry as a great hero and decided to remain a sightless, closed society, where only the Great Henry could stay. Thus, the nickname Henry for CAKE never reached the broader respects of the galaxies. Even so, Henry had landed the jackpot gold which spun both him and that dynamite, cool as cool gets, the one at the top, who everyone else copies but no one comes even close to cloning, CAKE to the top of the universe and beyond.

Once Sblitterdot decided (being blind they had no idea they were actually on neighboring Sblitterdot 2 and merely thought their houses were dodging them) to close their planet from all outsiders, they made a loving, heartfelt gesture to remove Henry's eyes as well. He quickly informed them he'd just received word he'd been transferred and must relocate immediately. Henry assured them all he'd miss them very much and a new CAKE representative would be along there soon to handle all their posotronic dogulet needs. (Wouldn't want a teenager to miss out on following his first dogulet.)

Henry did not wait around for the new salesman to arrive, leaving only a hasty note behind which said, "Sorry if you can't read this, Henry."

Lawology: Supposedly the study of Law, though no one can find a Lawologist to prove the theory since they became reclusive after their lost argument of the Theory of Relativity. It is generally an accepted principle that officials just make up the laws as they go along depending on what sounds good at the time, so no one has bothered to look for the Lawologists, finding it a much quieter Universe without them.

Lemurial Light Show: The Lemurial Light Shows are considered the most extravagant organic photon display in the known universe. Lemuria's do not have a home planet, but gather in a remote location in the empty space plains of Quadrant II. There, the beings comprised solely of light, commence with spawning. The act of laying fertilized eggs consumes both the male and female engaged in intercourse, emitting an explosion of sparkling photons which can be seen in nearby galaxies. Biologists claim the Lemurias give their lives to aid in the creation of their offspring, whereas Theoretical Biologists believe this is not the case at all and the Lemurias explode simply because the sex is that good. They have petitioned the Ultimate Galactic Headquarters for funds to study the matter further and determine if the same circumstance can occur in other life forms. There is a current waiting list to take part as subjects in the study, in which the Theoretical Biologists made sure to place their names at the top.

Ultimate Galactic Complaints and Returns Department: The Ultimate Galactic Headquarter, UGH, avowed ultimate war on complainers and returners across the known universe and declared by ultimate executive decree that anyone wishing to make a complaint against a sanctioned corporation must do so in person and freely submit themselves to the corporate complaint guidelines and be processed as an official complaint. Requests to return or replace items is considered a complaint and subject to the same guidelines. UGH further decreed the guidelines must be posted on lavatory doors just below the declaration stating all employees, assuming they have hands, must wash them at some point before returning to work, with a strong suggestion it be nearer their departure of the lavatory than their arrival.

Ultimate Galactic Headquarters: The Ultimate Galactic Headquarters is the literal and theoretical center of the known Universe. Since the Universe is ever expanding and new places are being discovered, that means it shifts around quite bit. In fact, it could pop up in almost any central quadrant at any given time, depending on how busy the explorers are or how lost a man can get before he is willing to ask for directions. It houses all branches and forms of government and law enforcement agencies, to include (but not limited to): The Galactic Complaints and Returns Department, The Classificationist Guild, The Acts of Stupidity Assessment Office, the Acts of Penile Stupidity Reprimandation and Castration Office, House of Internal Galactic Affairs and External Unknown Provisions Department, Good Deed Surcharge Facility, Spaceways, Triways and Wormhole Regulations and Upkeep Agency, The Psycho Waste Collection and Disposal Department, The Sherriff's Office and the Ultimate Galactic Headquarters Tax Authority. There are many more agencies, departments, offices, facilities, Guilds, people locked in closets and parrots that are also contained inside the Ultimate Galactic Headquarters. For the most part, the Tax Authority does the best business. It is frequently assumed there is no one in charge, as anyone who calls and asks to speak to the person in charge, is placed on hold indefinitely. In truth, Head of the Ultimate Galactic Headquarters is typically not found hiding in an undisclosed closet.

UGH Decree number 592743B2XY742.03: Specifically states that the Orchid Temple Motor Company, manufacturer of Starvettes, must include, as standard accessory, deflectors on all makes and models of its

Starvette product line, in all four tenses of the known universe. This decree was administered as a result of studies which showed drivers of Starvettes to be 1. Completely self-centered, and 2. As a result of number one, more likely to have accidents or damage other vehicles as they care more about where they are going than whether or not other cruisers may be already occupying that point in space and time, and 3. Also because of number one, are more likely to spend their funds repairing their own vehicle and not likely have any money left to fix anyone else's property they may have damaged as a result of one and two, but mostly one. Therefore, it was determined, if the Starvette owners did not need to repair their own cruiser, there would be money left to pay for the damage to everything else they had destroyed.

Universal Vadurian Approximate: In the infinite universe and in an infinite probability multi-universe time dimension, where not only is anything possible or probable, but actually is, then universal time approximations for ordering merchandise are infinite in nature. So if you ordered a book due out next month, you both never receive it and have already read it an infinite number of times.

Universal Q-tip: A highly effective tool to remove earwax. Most do not realize that Q-tips are actually a highly evolved race of hive dwelling beings. They have an exoskeleton stem like body and swirls of fluffy, tightly woven hair at each end of that body. Their small stature makes either end fit nicely into an ear canal, where the woven hair easily collects ample amounts of wax and debris. Q-tips feed on certain properties of ear wax. Once the Q-tip has successfully collected its quota and been thrown in the trash, it then opens a tiny, predestined, teleportation device containing a captured micro wormhole. It slips through the tear in space and returns to its home planet of Cotonia. There the Queen Cottonball oversees her busy workers as they produce food for the hive and help her raise the next generation of Q-tips.

Note of warning: Not all worker class Q-tips are happy with their lot and some have been known to bite their subjects. It is unclear where, exactly they keep their teeth. Others to be wary of are the musically inclined, as they like to play the eardrum and frequently become overzealous.

There have been many failed attempts to create an inorganic equivalent in the Universal marketplace. These ventures failed for two primary reasons. First: The living Q-tips seemed to work much better than their artificial counterparts because, evidently, people did not know how to clean their own ears properly, and Two: the Cotonians launched a spy campaign and infiltrated the bathrooms of the competitive corporate executives, puncturing their eardrums after morning showers. Thus any ideas for product improvement fell on deaf ears.

Sblitterdot: A small, presently uninhabited planet in a remote part of the galaxy with a great number of empty houses and buildings. Some corporations have considered purchasing the planet over the years to save costs on infrastructure but decided the commute was too long and the area too boring to commute to.

Sblitterdot 2: A planet in a remote part of the universe, neighboring Sblitterdot. There are also two more planets in that solar system not worth mentioning, so we won't. Sblitterdot 2 is inhabited by the people who built the houses on Sblitterdot, one. A CAKE representative and posotronic dogulets have taken over all official positions in their government. It is a closed society, but that does not really matter, as no one wants to go there anyway.

Geonozlings: The primary intelligent, sentient creatures originating from Geonozia. Geonozlings are easy to spot in a crowd because they have exactly too much nose. It is the prominent feature, where it, in fact, engulfs the whole of their faces. The Geonozlings take great pride in their large, bulbous protrusions, and the younger generations have begun investing large sums into surgical specialists to remove accidental features, such as eyes, lips, cheeks and other unsightly blemishes. The Geonozlings do not really need eyes as they seldom use the tiny round things located on each side of the nose bridge, which makes it impossible to see anything in front of them anyway, and it is a bit disorienting to see two sides but not the front, so most of the time they close their eyes anyway, as not to get dizzy. Only the medical specialists know exactly where their mouths are located, but it is assumed it is hidden somewhere below their tailored collars. As a deal to help get them outside their inverted sub-universe, the entire race contracted with UGH and make up the Internal Affairs Investigation Bureau. They are known for their thorough tenacity. They are also known for having the nastiest colds in the known universe.

Geonozia: a small planet located in an inverted sub-universe, where the galaxy is smaller than the solar system and the solar system a bit smaller than the planet and so on and so forth. It is thus not such a big deal to be a big fish in a small pond on Geonozia, the real trick is to even fit in the pond at all. The primary intelligent species heralding from Geonozia are the Geonozlings. They are not the only sentient species, but are recognized as the most intellectual because they were the only ones smart enough to move out into the primary universe where they could have a little more leg room. See Geonozlings.

Alterrean: A race of sentient beings. They are asexual and typically reproduce without the need for a partner. They generally identify themselves as either male or female, however the tradition is losing steam as the race evolves and is transcending the need for gender identity. The need for a partner and exhibiting a strong sex drive is considered an uncouth evolutionary throwback and parents frequently submit children exhibiting these symptoms for genetic alteration to repair the problem. Many genetic theoriticians believe this is the direct causation of the Fale movement, in which modern Altarrians have adopted a nongender designation, neither male nor female. It caused a bit of a linguistic problem at first, but the Classification Guild quickly drew up and adopted a series of nouns and pronouns to reflect the change. The Classification Guild determined that in reality, Alterrians were both male and female, rather than neither, as they are capable of reproduction and reproduction does require a sexual act. Even if it is alone. The new classification names the gender as Fale (a combination of male and female which represents the aforementioned, along with boy/girl, man/woman, gentleman/lady, dude/chick, etc.) and the pronouns are Fe (he/she), Fis (his/hers), and Fim (him/her). Also noted are the noun roles in a family: Foth (parent), Font (son/daughter) and Fotter (sibling designation, brother/sister), Func (aunt/uncle), Fothing (grandparent). Example in a sentence: A young fale asked fim foth if fe could borrow fim fotter's sweater because fe had lost fis at their func's loft when the neighbor's spoiled font threw it off the balcony.

Anti-Paradoxical Event: a moment in the time continuum, or an event, which is definitive and stubbornly does not change. It is a constant across all universes, dimensions, and timelines where those circumstances are capable of arising. For instance, say your life is defined by marrying your high school sweetheart, but then you find out they are less sweet and more a horrible, annoying, nagging, and generally unpleasant being once married. You may try taking a couch back to warn yourself not to marry the jerk, give dire warnings, attempt reason or even intervention. If it is an anti-paradoxical event, no amount of interference will change the fact that you get married and it is horrible. The only way to change the event is to create a planetary circumstance where it cannot occur, such as traveling back and destroying all life on the planet prior to evolutionary advances substantial enough for any individual to avoid destruction, and destruction of the planet and solar system, itself. UGH has strict laws against such actions without written consent and a rather expensive destruction zoning permit. While most educated persons accept this is the scientific balance that everything is possible, including the possibility that some things cannot be changed, gossip columns amongst deities suggest that Destiny and Fate had teamed up in a joint lawsuit against Chaos and Probability. Nature had mediated the conflict and agreed upon the anti-paradoxical event as a sound compromise to ensure no one's rights were impeded.

Annoyance: Annoyance is another Universal Constant used by scientists and theoretical scientists which helps establish the measurable passage of time and events through the fabric of the universe. The universal second, time constant, is measured by a constant drum beat. The annoyance constant is measured by the irritation of the neighbors of the man constantly beating his drum.

Classification Theoreticist: One who theorizes the impact of Classification lists, also known as Classification Critics. According to the Classification Guild, these do not exist.

Classificationist Guild: 1. Guild sanctioned by the Ultimate Galactic Headquarters to classify all things in the universe, making sure everything has a name, a general description by which to recognize it and an order categorizing it with other similar things in the known Universe. Since the Ultimate Galactic Universe is infinite, there are infinite objects in it, therefore the Classificationist Guild puts priority on identifying only those things for which there is submitted a proper work order to identify it along with subsequent funds to research the query. The Guild refuses to acknowledge the existence of any person, place or thing until these terms are met and the results of the order determined. This was a great resource for Insurance companies trying to get out of paying for damages to items that are specifically and individually identified by the Classificationist Guild, stating they do not exist. This practice led to item specific requests for houses at distinct addresses, particular vehicles of transport, jewelry, husbands, wives, pets, couches and doorknobs, until such time as the highly annoyed Classificationist Guild made an Ultimate Universal Proclamation that, in fact, Insurance companies did not exist. With that, all the insurance companies vanished and the problem was solved. 2. As defined by the Ultimate Galactic Dictionary: a snobby group of self-proclaimed scientists who spend their time compiling large lists of things for money and producing a wholly incomplete dictionary, solely comprised of what they've been paid to make lists of. They spend a lot of time stamping about demanding things stop trying to exist until they are properly written down.

CAKE: The largest sanctioned or unsanctioned corporation in all four tenses of the known universe. It is a monstrosterous business entity so resoundedly huge in size that its billing department encompasses three star systems. It is known by many nick names such as The Big Co, God and Company, and as Henry by a small sector in Zeta Quaq on a planet known as Sblitterdot. But few people travel to Zeda Quaq and even fewer go on from there to Sblitterdot.

CAKE Complaints and Returns Policy: After an internal expenditure audit, CAKE discovered it could save a zillion and a half Vadurian Credits a year by simply shooting the first person in line at the customer service desk. While a few Sympatheticists disguised as Associate Vice Presidents argued this would hurt their bottom line because sound business theory said dead customers were not, typically, repeat customers, the more dominant and higher paid Practicologists, undisguised as Senior Vice Presidents, pointed out that an unhappy customer was unlikely to buy anything else anyway. The Sympatheticists, feeling a losing battle, and after a few legal wrangles, unsuccessful hunger strikes and staring contests finally won a concession over a definitive game of checkers. The compromise greatly annoyed the Practicologists, but they finally agreed to scrap the savings on returned items and replace, refund or offer and in-store coupon to those who presented a valid receipt. The Sympatheticists insisted this should happen before they are shot so the customer can die satisfied with their service, but this argument did not hold. If they were going to take the time to resolve the problem before they shot the customer, there would be no point in shooting anyone, just another expense to an already ridiculously expensive system. The Sympatheticists were forced to slump away with what they could. The Practicologists grumbled a bit about the concession to make refunds, exchanges or any other rubbish to someone who couldn't even use it, but decided it was cheaper than continuing the legal expenditures. And a wager over a game of checkers is smart on difficult to overthrow in court. Therefore, once verified, the item, refund or in-store coupon would be mailed to the closest living relative. However, the Practicologists insisted the next of kin must pick up the shipping costs and processing fees (which include such things as paper and copy expenses, ammunition charges and the cost of a small but tasteful cremation ceremony).

Couch: A sofa. A piece of furniture generally utilized in the social or family gathering area of a home or office. They can sometimes be found in waiting rooms. It is also the central element of time travel. Based on the theory of Relativity (See Theory of Relativity) the couch is the governing instrument by which time is commanded. While the Theory of Relativity initially interjects the distortion of time based on the relative sleeping on the couch, the constant remains the couch and, when manipulated properly, can be utilized to jump through primordial strings of time and space. While any couch can accomplish this, it is suggested a nice comfortable couch is much better. It is more tasteful than, say an orange, brown and purple striped couch with daisies and paisley prints on the cushions. It also makes for a much more pleasant ride while your atoms are ripped apart and slapped back together in a near proximity of the place they once occupied. Always know who has slept on the couch most recently and whether or not they were slobs. Couches frequently redeposit stains and unwelcomed blemishes from themselves and onto their unsuspecting passengers during microshifts. They have also been known to sprout potatoes if left idle for too long.

Chaos: In theory, chaos is a state of being without conformity, rules, or structure. In reality, Chaos is a sexy goddess-like incarnation who likes to throw wild twists into other god-like incarnation's handiwork. She frequently does this by seducing them and dropping little hints about what might get her excited and, therefore, help the god-like incarnation to get really lucky. An excellent example of her work are the Bzertani. She is a very bad girl and thoroughly enjoys her lot in the universe.

Flaming Vodka: distilled from the volcanic potatoes of Zeti tri-Dai, it is the second highest concentration of alcohol in the known universe. Just a few drops added to a martini and it must be lit on fire to bring the concentration down to nonlethal dosage. The drink has been banned from the two civilized quadrants in the Ultimate Universe. Those two quadrants petitioned the others to do the same, whereby, in the only political action to ever gain the full support of their communities, the politicians told the do-gooders to go suck off, as they didn't care to be civilized if it meant they couldn't get a good drink.

Yoga: A small, dusty planet located in Quadrant XXV. The Planet has only one indigenous life form, the Yogalarians. There are no trees, animals, insects or marine life. In fact, there is no water for marine life to exist. Yoga and the Yogalarians have been a real kick in the pants for Evolution Theoreticists throughout the known Universe. Whenever and Evolutionist has an argument with a Supreme Dietyologist, it usually turns ugly with the Dietyologist eventually chanting, "Yoga. Yoga. Yoga," and someone ends up sticking out there tongue just before the fist fight ensues, where then the Evolutionist says, "Maybe if you had evolved your self-preservation skills a bit more, you wouldn't be getting your face smashed in." Yoga has nothing to trade, no precious, semi-precious or even remotely interesting resources of value to anyone, including the Yogalarians. There is only one trade occupation. Yoga is the Bookie Capitol of the Ultimate Galactic Universe.

How did this come about? The Yogalarians are a swarthy, clever race and had survived and thrived despite all natural, physical and scientific laws which demanded they should not exist. They looked Evolution in the eye and said, "Double or nothing," and won. They beat the odds against their survival with confident ease and figured it was a quality they could share with the universe. Beware the Guaranteed Sure-to-win clause in fine print when placing a bet with a Yogalarian Bookie, as it does not necessarily impart who will win, but explicitly states the winner will most likely not be the person placing the wager.

Yogalarian: Race of large people from the planet Yoga. Yogalarians head and control the Ultimate Galactic Universe Bookie Guild. This is helped by the fact that they are large, huge really, and intimidating, born with bulky muscles, heavy eyebrows and a grimace. The muscles get bulkier, the eyebrows thicker and the grimace more scowling as they age to maturity. See Yoga.

Reen'os: the dominant, intelligent, sentient , feline species of the planet Kultren in Quadrant XVIII. *See also Kultren.* Reen'os (which is both singular and plural, like fish but not fish) typically are distinguished by their light blue fur, which ranges from long and shaggy to short and sleek. They are known to be extremely intelligent and cunning, and highly skilled in combat. They celebrate the warlike traditions of their ancestors, though UGH treaties and the threat of a spade and neuter program prevent them from invading and pillaging other systems. Most off planet Reen'os work either as criminals or bounty hunters as it suits their fast paced penchant for violence and trickery. They hate to be called Huma-kitties. Seriously, never call one that. Not only will they kill you, they will take a couch back in time to kill you again before you died the first time.

Red: A primary color of the rainbow and prism. Second cousin to Purple and Orange. A notable third cousin is Brown. Also incestuously related to Scarlet, Maroon, Burgundy, Violet Red, Pink, Crimson and Red-orange. There are some suggestions it may be tangled in somewhere with Fuchsia and Tangerine as well. In the color family, it is the most reviled, known to snicker at the others and agitate family gatherings. Yellow simply refuses to be seen with Red any more. It is also the first color to be tried and convicted in a court of galactic law for stalking. It showed up in court but took the fifth and said nothing in its own defense, which went a long way to making it look guilty. A restraining order was awarded to the plaintiff, whereby directing Red not to come within visual sight of the offended party, or frequent any location the victim is at or is likely to be, (See Beology) under penalty of law. Failure to comply would result in incarceration. Attorneys for Red argued that the penalty was impractical because how were authorities supposed to detain and incarcerate a color? The judge declared that was a problem for Law Enforcement to figure out.

The legal issues did not end with the judge's final gavel tap, however, as accusations of color profiling began to emerge. Scarlet, Crimson and Cherry all filed separate Police Harassment suits stating they were unfairly targeted and detained for merely resembling Red. There is a current injunction against color profiling and all colors are now required to carry proof of their identity.

Evolution: In theory, evolution is the progression of a living thing from single cell to multi cell, to walking or swimming to recognizing it is hungry and then figuring out how to not be hungry, and so on. In reality, Evolution is a pretty easily distracted, god-like artisan with an attention deficit disorder, attempting to create the perfect species. He has many projects going at all times, spreading his attention thin, resulting in a few forgotten specimens scattered about. He tends to be somewhat shy but can be easily influenced by a lady god-like entity showing him a bit of attention, and create some exquisitely beautiful creature for her to enjoy. However, these tend to be fairly unbalanced and die out rather quickly. Creationism says Evolution is all show and no substance.

Neros: An abandoned planet in Quadrant XXVIII. It consists mostly of salty water with just the peaks from its many underwater mountain ranges breaking the oceanic surface. The planet gets its purplish glow from a luminescent microorganism exclusive to the oceans of Neros. The previous inhabitants, Nerelons, have a severe dislike for procrastination. Thus, when they discovered their planet would eventually be destroyed when the sun it orbits goes super nova (due to happen in about ten billion years) they decided to not just wait around. They loaded up and left Neros behind. Nature has since reclaimed their underwater cities and swimming with the sharks of Neros has become a favorite patch to claim among adventure seekers and star prophets.

Nerelons: The amphibious species originating from Neros is Quadrant XXVIII but currently residing on Pot in Quadrant I. While the official story is that the Nerelons left their home planet as a precaution against the eventual, predicted demise of both their sun and Neros, some speculate it had more to do with the fact that they prefer living in underwater cities and the oceans of Neros are home to the most dangerous, deadly, lethal and downright unfriendly sharks in the known universes. The sharks enjoyed Nerelon snacks between meals of Nerelon, who have few natural defenses.

Bar-b-que Pit: Open fire in a large hole dug in the earth used in more primitive cultures as a resource for cooking various animal, fish or avian parts for the purpose of sustenance. Used in sophisticated cultures when they want to feel less advanced and get in touch with their more primitive instincts to cook various animal, fish or avian body parts over open fires. This is usually done in conjunction with the consumption of copious amounts of intoxicating beverages, which helps to devolve the brain function and get everyone in a more primitive mood.

Bordagrean Roses: A carnivorous shrubbery producing luscious rose blossoms with such enticing aromas as to attract gardeners from all across the known universe. The Bordagrean Roses are the sole intelligent life form on Bordag, found in Quadrant XI in the Doomie Star System. The entire planet is covered in lush gardens of these shrubberies. Many attempts to excavate the hedges have failed, mostly because the persons attempting to do the excavating were eaten. The planet has since become a tourist trap for adventurists who run through the garden trails naked, dodging thorny vines whipping out to snare them. The roses have not complained as it gives them a steady source of imported food products, though they prefer gardeners over naked adventure seekers. The coveralls lend fiber to their diet and help in the digestive process.

Brick Wilson:
Hair: Dark, wavy and almost always neatly positioned upon his head, except when he is drunk, in which case it flounders about and tries to crawl away, so he is constantly slapping his head to keep it still when he drinks.
Eyes: Bluish, greenish, hazelish, purplish, depending on the light
Skin: clear, caramel

Features: handsome, but not nearly as handsome as
Brick thinks he is
Height: average, not too tall, not too short, perfect for
walking through doors and sleeping on beds without
hanging off and sitting in chairs without his legs
dangling.
Body style: humanoid, meaning a head at the top, set
on a neck, above shoulders, from which extend two
arms and a trunk housing vital organs. The trunk is held
up by two legs fixated to two feet, one on each leg.
The arms have one hand each. The left hand has four
fingers, the right hand has five, four natural and one
prosthetic pinky. Brick cannot afford a prosthetic pinky
for his left hand at the moment. He is equipped with
male anatomy which, in fact, does have an actual brain
of its own and an override mechanism to subdue the
more logically oriented brain housed in his head. This is
the ultimate reason why he lost his job as it is never a
good idea to forget to wear a penile brainwave
inhibitor condom while working. Such actions are
frequently subject to an Ultimate Penile Stupidity fine.
Features: Broad, crooked smile and smallish ears he
hides beneath carefully manicured hair. Thin but not
skinny, strong enough but not a body builder. The
crooked smile is a result of being slapped so hard in a
bar that it shifted his face slightly, but it is most
notable when he smiles. He has a peculiar tattoo of a
diamond inside a circle inside a square on his left
shoulder that he cannot remember getting. He was not
drunk, at least not that time, it simply appeared one
day somewhere between his morning shower and

shave. He shrugged it off, figuring stranger things had happened and maybe he could use it to pick up women.

Habits: Tapping his prosthetic pinky on hard surfaces to make an annoying clicking noise. Bad pick-up lines.

Dislikes: Irrational fear of the color red. The first person in the galaxy to successfully obtain a restraining order against a color. He routinely attempts to have the offending color apprehended by authorities.

Likes: Not wearing a penile brainwave inhibitor condom when working

Lives: Lives in quadrant XXXV, the slum quadrant of the universe, in a high rise, cheap domicile complex with an overlooking view of a Giant Glebular Succor Worm reservation. A much different habitat than he had when he was an up and coming special agent for the Ultimate Galactic Headquarters. He'd once had viduries to waste, a nice, rotating domicile pad perfect for impressing ladies and an expense account to impress them with. Now he lives with his dysfunctional android secretary model, Sally Sirkuts in a three room habitat: a bedroom, a living room and a kitchen bathroom combination unit. Living has taken a downhill turn.

Interests and hobbies: drinking too much and slapping his hair, attempting to pick up women and go back to their place because he hates his and hopes he will eventually forget where he lives and never go back. Annoying people who do not give him what he wants.

Beologist: One who studies Beology.

Beology: /bee' aw law gee/ The study of being and, more specific, how and where one is being. The most prominent theory deduces that because one could be at any place at any given time, then one is likely to be at any place at any given time.

Beology Theoreticist: One who thinks of new ways to study Beology.

Jugnugs: Jugnugs hail from the planet Jugnu in Quadrant III. They are the only life form from this planet. As sentient rock formations, Jugnuts began traveling the universes fairly early in their evolution. They move by telekinesis, have no respiratory or circulatory system, can survive in many extreme conditions and gain nutrients through osmosis when soaking in water saturated dirt, also known as mud. Many Jugnugs are mistaken for asteroids floating about in space. It is unknown exactly how they reproduce or if they just simply break into smaller pieces. They range in color based on their primary diet from sorted russets to gold to hints of blue and green under normal conditions.

Dilani: Planet located in Quadrant II. The Dilanians were the first or second known species to be detrimentally effected by time travel, depending on which theoretical ideology one chooses to side with. They are the first species to successfully sue and receive compensation for a temporal accident. At some point in the future or past (the exact time and location is sealed by court order to prevent further tampering and a continuation of mucking things about by attempting to prevent the instance which should not have happened in the first place. Unless of course, it was meant to happen, and that gets into a whole other ball field of theoretics, which gave the judge a headache, so he shut everyone up, dismissed for lunch and had several dinks to clear his head before coming back and telling everyone what they were going to do. So, again, at some point in the future or past there was an industrial accident involving a couch, the fulcrum of the time warp, an egg beater and a gene splicer at the Beat A Better Egg Corporation research and development facility. The thought was that the best beaten egg was one that came already beaten in the shell. This idea was either later or earlier developed into reality with the help of the company's CEO's niece who took up temporary residence on the family's couch. The damage inflicted on the Dilanians proved permanent, where the entire population, one millions years ago, suddenly had no pinky fingers, the script having been deleted from their DNA sequence. Many lawsuits ensued. Most placed by wealthy Dilanian Coconut Plantation owners and Tourqi Hen Farmers. The judge awarded those originally sustaining the injury be compensated in a currency acceptable to their present, or past rather, culture. He ordered the Beat A Better Egg Corporation to immediately pay, one million years ago, to each injured party (which included all Dilanians living on the planet at the actual time the missing digits occurred) three torque hens, ten pretty blue rocks and twenty coconuts. This was considered reasonable compensation for their loss, given the value of these items at that point in history. The hens and coconuts were purchased from present Dilanian plantations and farms and the rocks were picked up off the ground from and undisclosed location.

Some Theoreticists believe the first species adversely effected by a time warp is the Pesnort, or Ptyridactoplatimus, which became extinct distinctly before the Dilanians lost their pinkies. But because the additional, accidental slaughter of ten thousand spontaneously appearing Pesnorts actually coincides exactly with the historical extinction of the species, other Theoreticists claim that it was merely nature righting itself and thereby the time warp committed no harm or foul by letting Nature make sure it did its job properly.

Dimensionology: the scientific and religious study of the omni-dimensional universe.

Dave's Drive-thru Donut Planet: The vastly popular Dave's Drive-thru Donut Planet was purchased by the once small and little known Dave's Donuts. The planet was very cheap, as it has no atmosphere and was considered post-apocalyptic defunct planetary rubble. Larry, the owner and pioneer of Dave's Donuts, took out a hefty loan to clear away the rubble surrounding the planet and have it hauled off to surround other planets, which was highly controversial, since this created what some referred to as rubble overcrowding in designated rubble zones. But those people were deemed unfit to lodge complaints because they were, as a matter of ethics, determined to disagree with most everything. Therefore, their discontent was ignored. Larry's supporters pointed out that the rubble had been completely silent on the issue and if it felt overcrowded, it should say something. This consensus was upheld by a majority of the public and Larry was allowed to finish construction of his donut empire. What made the planet perfect for Larry's designs was its peculiar shape. Unlike most planetary objects which are roundish and spherical, this planet had suffered a cataclysmic event, leaving a giant hole directly through its core. In essence, what was left intact of the planet looked like a floating donut is space. It had been an unruly eyesore to those in Quadrant XXIV for eons, but no one wanted to spend the tax revenue to clean up the mess. Collectively the planets of Quadrant XXIV decided to place the planet up for auction in hopes some idiot would buy it cheap and then they could hold him to zoning laws and insist he clean up the mess. The plan worked beautifully, as Larry, having a keen eye for a business opportunity, agreed to purchase the property and clean it up so long as the Quadrant XXIV bank agreed to give him the loan to do it. Larry's credit had been a bit shaky since his sixteenth divorce from his third wife (some things have a hard time sticking) so he bought the planet for five thousand Viduries and commenced the five billion Vidurie clean up. The bank was not so keen on giving Larry the loan, but the overwhelming public opinion and swift legislation stating that anyone purchasing a demolished planet in Quadrant XXIV is entitled to and cannot be denied a loan for whatever sum it requires to clean it up and transform it into something functional and less unattractive, rather forced the issue. They succumbed to the political, legal and community pressure, along with the bank president who said moon real estate (which he recently acquired) would triple in value with the mess cleaned up.

Dave's is the only drive-thru donut planet in the Ultimate Galactic Universe. It sells coffee mugs saying, "I drove through Dave's big hole!" and t-shirts, plastic bobble donuts for the dash, pencil sets, refrigerator magnets, collectible spoons, thimbles, hats, caps, glasses, toasters, oversized remote controls, piñatas, stuffed animals, erasers, cup cozies, handbags, wallets, laser pens, temporary tattoos, and on Tuesdays between four and seven, you can even get donuts.

See also: Plaid

Dorvanian Torture Technique: Developed by the Kulus Tribe and named after their most infamous leader, Dorvan. The Kulus would capture rival tribe members and submit them to heinous torture, placing them in tents with mediocre lighting, uncomfortable furnishing, stale food and bad beverages until they succumbed to boredom so complete, they would do or say anything to break the monotony.

Detective Legal Prosecution Exclusion Topics: A list of topics for which laws under the topics may be rendered null and void when broken by a license detective with special clearance, and in the scope of services to a client under contract. Exclusions are at the discretion of the UGH Judiciary Oversight Committee for Special Private Agents and can be extended to such offenses as murder, theft, breaking and entering, destruction of property, and intentionally leaving chewing gum on public benches and sidewalks.

Hilep Schitter/Hilep/Schitter: Previously known as Hilep Schitter, the business tycoon with more money than anyone knows, since it literally cannot be counted, is the first and only being in the Ultimate Galactic Universe to divorce himself. The divorce was based on irreconcilable differences and in the decree Hilep, the first name, retained the right half of the body. The last name, Schitter, was awarded the left half. The various personality traits were distributed on what the judge determined was a reasonable platform. Hilep kept most of the compassion and Schitter was awarded the criminal intent. Because much of the wealth was a result of criminal activity, Hilep was granted the majority of wealth. They split the greed fifty-fifty. Many economic theoreticists suggested the divorce was a clever ruse contrived to legitimize the Schitter fortune and prevent an UGH Tax Authority seizure of assets. Due to Schitter's criminal nature,

Hilep was given sole custody of their daughter and Schitter's parental rights were terminated.

MORE RUMORS ABOUT THE AUTHOR

It is rumored that Marq Truong is, in fact, a fictional science fiction author in a larger novel someone else is writing. It is also rumored the rest of us are characters in that story as well. ~ A dubias, anonymous account copied from a lavatory wall in Quadrant II

It is rumored Marq Truong is so incredibly cool that each morning he paraglides from his mountain abode, treks across a vast wilderness of exotic and dangerous creatures, forages for sustenance and drinks from the river of creativity. Of course, some say he more likely stumbles out of bed and down the stairs in a bathrobe, tripping over the cat and groggily feels his way to the coffee pot before even bothering to open his eyes to grab yesterday's left over doughnut. ~ Frederica LaDavorie who alleges to have heard this in her travels into the uncharted Quadrants.

It is rumored that Marq Truong comes from a distant, logical universe and writing Brick Wilson is how he copes with the shock of finding himself stranded here. ~ From a source who wishes to remain anonymous.

It is rumored that Marq Truong is actually a middle-aged, suburban housewife with purple hair, two dogs and three cats, living a vicarious double life as the only author insane enough to turn a color into an antagonist. ~ An anonymous middle-aged suburban housewife in a presently undisclosed location.

It is rumored Marq Truong lives on a small, secluded island in the Florida Keys on a planet in the uncharted Quadrants, where he subsists on canned tins of tuna and tomatoes, wears a large hat and plays bongo drums while he writes. ~ Tanja Thumbersnork, Quadrant IX

The Department on Theoretical Rumorology would like to submit, in collaboration with the Beology and Theoretical Beology Institutes, that based on the infinite nature of the universe, time and dimensions, all rumors which theoretically could exist, do, in fact, exist and that further, the existence of a rumor indicates the existence of a potential reality. Since all potential realities theoretically exist, and based on theoretical beology, anything that theoretically exists, does exist, then the conclusion is that all rumors are simultaneously true, including the rumor that Marq Truong does not exist at all and neither do we or anyone else. ~ Angrilika Banderbum, Director, The Department of Rumorology

Excerpt From
The Universe Sucks: Existence is Futile
By Elona Schitter
Reluctantly Edited by Marq Truong

CHAPTER ONE
POETRY ABOUT STARS

1.0 Hot

Stars are hot.
Very hot.
They blast with unforgiving heat
and incinerate the bodies of flesh
which dare to dive too close.
Except for Salamandoreans.
They are rumored to live inside suns, but no one
knows.
Is incineration a good way to die?
Everything dies.
Almost everything.
Everything that doesn't die
is trapped in this miserable existence for eternity.
I'd rather fly into the sun
and dance with a Salamandorean.
Then die.
But I won't get to
because the stupid sun will
incinerate me
first.

1.1 Light

The infinite stars and star systems
cannot light all of space
which, too, is infinite.
Which doesn't make sense.
If there is infinite space and infinite light
then how can there be darkness?
But the darkness is infinite, too.
Or we don't know the difference between the light and
the dark
and it is really just
space.
The darkness is within us
the light is what we wish we could touch.
And the space goes on forever.
… the light always just out of our reach.

1.2 Were they?

They were bright and beautiful
gleaming rays of hope in the night sky
that promised a child
adventure
with visions of exploration and excitement.
Or were they conniving demons at play
soliciting the souls of the innocent
with lies of what the universes hold?
The stars claimed to be your friend,
but,
were they?

1.3 Ugh

Not UGH, Ugh.
I hate stars.
Pretending to be all glittery.
From a distance they dazzle
but the closer you get
the hotter and sweatier
you become
until you stink.
Then they cook
your flesh
and devour you,
reducing your corpse
to its most base component.
Then solar winds whisk
you away,
fodder to eternity's
endless course of destruction.

1.4 Vespers

kissed by the first
vespers
of the night sky
on a distant world
only few have touched
and sinking in solemn loneliness
as it is only the
light of
that distant sun
which found you
and saw the darkness inside.
But its simple, flickering light
was not enough
to fill
the void
that childish hope
had abandoned.

1.5 They are Idiots

"Look to the stars," they said.
Idiots.
"Let the stars be your guide," they said.
Idiots.
"Shoot for the stars," they said.
Idiots.
"Reach for the stars," they said.
Idiots.
Do they even know that stars
are giant balls of unstable gases
burning at billions of degrees?
Idiots.

1.6 Motion Sickness

Everything moves
The stars are not fixed into place
but fluid
and spinning
a death spiral
simultaneously
flinging all of
the universe away
and sucking it in.
We cannot escape
the push and pull
of the universal dance.
Come here
Go there
Be this
Do that
we are spinning
in circles of confusion
unable to grasp the beat of the music
or find rhythm
to steady ourselves.
Unable to feel reason.
We spin until
the illness of it consumes us.

1.7 Happy Sunshine

Yeah. You wish.
The sun is not happy.
None of them are happy.
They don't make you happy.
They do not feel or express feelings.
They do not react to your emotions.
For all the heat they thrash into the universes
their hearts are cold.

1.8 Sun of a Bitch

Because there actually is
a sun
that belongs
to a female
dog.
My father
bought his dog,
Lulu,
a small,
blue sun
in Quadrant IV.
Which makes it
the
Sun of a Bitch.
I found it
poetic.
But I still
hate
that
spoiled
dog.

1.9 No Stars

were there no stars
there would be no light
there would be no planets teeming with life
no ships zipping about space
no fashionable donut planet
no frat boys interrupting
when someone they assume is female
speaks
no infinite corporate battles
over the flavors of soda
and no mind numbing professors
indoctrinating young minds
to think as they are told to think
-which is to not think at all.
There would be darkness.
And in that darkness
a profound silence
and peace.
Suns.
We could do without them.
It would save everyone time.
It is easier
not to think for yourself
when you don't exist

(End of Excerpt)

BOOKS IN THE BRICK WILSON SERIES

Brick Wilson: For Hire (Book One)
Marq Truong

Brick Wilson's adventure takes the reader crashing through universes, galaxies, circuits, and alternate realities where anything can and does happen. On his search for the lost (or was it stolen?) Pesnort, Brick is continually challenged by dangers real and imagined as he skillfully avoids the Ultimate Galactic Headquarters Tax Authority, dodges the increasingly menacing plots for his demise by arch nemesis Terd Murchison, and is continually stalked and mocked by the color Red. Can he save the Pesnort, the universe and himself with a psychotic android in tow? Brick invites everyone to tag along on his chaotic ride through the Ultimate Galactic Universe. Cheers.

The Universe Sucks: Existence Is Futile
(companion)
Elona Schitter
Reluctantly edited by Marq Truong

Elona Schitter takes the reader on a dark and disturbing emotional journey through her depressing view of the Ultimate Galactic universe. She makes no apologies for, "...just telling it like I see it."

The editor, Marq Truong, says, "I had so many tequila shots reading this I ran out of limes. This is poetry at its worst. Elona channels Depression-incarnate."

Coming soon in the Brick Wilson Series:

Brick Wilson: Slightly Off Center
Marq Truong

Return to the Ultimate Galactic Universe on another chaotic adventure with Brick Wilson, Jagger, Ivy and a lot of pineapples. And a camel. But not a camel eating pineapples.

Thunder Paw
Marq Truong

Traipse through the Ultimate Universe with a blue mercenary cat pirate, Thunder Paw, and his ancestral quest to find the legendary planet Flatonia.

FIND MORE INFORMATION ABOUT
THE ULTIMATE GALACTIC UNIVERSE,
BRICK WILSON,
EVENTS, CONTESTS,
AND
ADVENTURE GEAR
AT THE OFFICIAL WEBSITE!

ULTIMATEGALACTICUNIVERSE.COM
AND
BRICKWILSON.COM

BE SURE TO CHECK THE LEELOO PUBLISHING
OFFICIAL WEBSITE FOR THESE AND MORE
GREAT TITLES AT

LEELOOPUB.COM

Dragon Bloode: Covet
By Mishka Williams

Dragons. Once a mighty race of winged gods, they're reduced to three. No longer do they resemble the scaled Flying marvels of their ancestry, but the humans who interbred with their ForeFathers.
The Bloode is thin and dying.
The Draak Empire is rife with division between its human Emperor and Dragon generals.
Dive into a world rich with magic, Dragons, and lust.

Edge of Ridiculous
Anne Coffer

She's human. He's not.
For the most part. We're pretty sure.
Maybe a little human... humanoid at least.
George isn't her real name. Bob isn't his.
When fate intervenes on the loop in Lubbock,
Texas, nothing will be the same for George
again. Her fantasies of a fairytale adventure
come true. Except for the part with the
monsters. And the jail time.
And the absolute vomit inducing terror of
creating an online dating profile.

Samiyah
L.R. Hicks

Samiyah is the ideal human woman. She lives on the ranch, the best place to buy human stock in the galaxy cluster. For years she trains to be the best sex slave money can buy. Now, the time has come for her to leave with her new master. She begs her friend, the old Parishioner, to help her escape. When he does, her expectations disappear with the only life she has ever known. Adventure, alien relics, and love of different spectrums await her.

Letters: Margaret Florence Baine
By Ann Lavendar

Maggie's story begins in 1898 with a series of letters written to her close cousin who has traveled West with her family. The five years of letters depict the journey of a young woman of privilege as she discovers the triumphs and tribulations of love, life and self discovery. The reader experiences a unique and deep perspective as they watch her grow from the girl she was taught to be into the woman she chooses to become.

Letters: Evelyn Rose Whitten
By Ann Lavendar

Eve's story begins in 1948 when she is just turning seventeen. Though still in High School, she finds herself in a heated romance leaving her needing a hasty marriage. One moment she is a school girl and the next a married woman with a child on the way. Facing ever more trials and decisions, her life is a raging tempest she fights to master but cannot contain. Witness her struggle through a series of letters as she strives to discover herself and determine which means more, love or honor.

Soon to release titles from

LeeLoo Publishing™

Dragon Bloode: Rebirth
By Mishka Williams
To release November 2018

Return to the gothic Fantasy world of Alperin in the sequel to Williams' highly acclaimed debut novel, Dragon Bloode: Covet.

Puppies
By Jed Wood
To release September 2018

Love is a dangerous affair, even for the Devil, himself.

Cheers!